For
Sarah

Mr. Overby is Falling

A novella

by

Nathan Tyree

PublishAmerica
Baltimore

First printing

ISBN: 1-4137-1526-5
PUBLISHED BY PUBLISHAMERICA, LLLP
www.publishamerica.com
Baltimore

Printed in the United States of America

"It is possible to provide security against other ills,but as far as death is concerned, we men live in a city without walls."

-Epicurus

"God is dead."

-Nietzsche

Something Like A Prologue

None of this is real. None of this matters. It's not on TV, so you can just ignore it. If it's not on TV, it's not real anyway. This is where I find myself.

Standing there, the blood forming sticky little pools around my shoes, I can see that it is soaking into the soft cowhide, ruining the leather. There's a lot of it. God, who knew that a person could have so much blood in them?

He's lying there; that big blood factory leaking all over my nice, new shoes that I haven't even gotten broken in yet. They're still stiff. Still hard. And he looks like a big pile of dirty laundry, all crumpled up and forgotten on the floor. There's way too much of him. He's huge. A massive, unmade bed thrown about on the cold, damp floor and bleeding everywhere. He's trying to say something, so I lean down to listen. He croaks something I can't make out. I lean in closer. He lifts a bloody hand to touch my face. It leaves a sickly smear of blood, and he says:

But wait. But all that's later. All of these things that aren't on TV came after. Before I tell you what he said, I have to tell you this. First:

Mr. Overby on the Edge of the Empire

The second law of thermodynamics states that the universe is in an increasing state of entropy. Or, as Yeats so aptly put it: "Things fall apart". We know this better than most, living, as we do, on the edge of the empire. Perhaps at the heart of Rome they didn't realize that their great state was crumbling; but out around the periphery you could see the edges beginning to fray; to unravel. I am seeing it again. But this time it's not just Rome that has felt the spark, the whole of humanity is coming apart before my eyes and I can barely wait.

How could I be so lucky? I don't know. I guess it boils down to being in the right moment. I can't take any credit for that. I had no hand in the time of my birth. I was born in winter, which is no surprise. Most Manic Depressives are born in winter or fall. The doctors don't know what this means, but, they assure me it means something. The doctors are always telling me things.

Winter is the cruel season. It strips; it lays waste to life, denuding the earth, leaving the cold white of bare bone and ice. Winter, it seems, will never end. It comes like plague and moves across the mind and the land.

Winter is the season of despair. The suicide rate skyrockets in winter. It grows steadily toward its peak, which comes on Christmas day. All those happy children rushing downstairs to open festive packages clothed in multicolored paper while just beyond their sight thousands succumb to the double-edged grin of the razor, or the handful of pills chased with gin, or the revving car engine in an enclosed space.

So it is chance that put me here, at the end of the world with the ability to appreciate and understand it. I am the only one to chronicle the decline and fall of humanity. I don't call it civilization. There is no such thing as civilization, and even if there is it has nothing to do with me.

The Strong Force

I first started to see it when I was very young. It was all around me, but I didn't know what I was witnessing. Without knowing the importance of what I was seeing, I quietly watched the true end of the world, the calm precursor to the climax that everyone would recognize.

When our sun goes, the Earth will be dead for eight minutes before anyone knows it. It will take the event that long to travel the distance. The heat, the blast wave of a Nova will begin all those cold miles away and at that moment we will all be dead. Corpses walking, singing, eating, fucking, smoking, sleeping for eight minutes before the heat turns us to ash where we stand. Those eight minutes will be meaningless; just as the last twenty-seven years have been meaningless. Ashes. Ashes and rubble.

I watched the world end in 1973, and I have been waiting for the blast wave ever since. I have been waiting patiently for the heat to cross all those cold, dead, empty miles to turn us to ash and rubble where we stand. Again, ashes and rubble.

She was walking in her own neighborhood, a hundred yards from the warmth of her door and the safety it offered when he approached her. It wasn't night. There was no cover of darkness. No pool of shadow to conceal the creature moving toward her. The sun was high and strong and bright as it looked down on the young woman and the man who would kill her.

He did not rob her. She had nearly thirty dollars in her purse, but he never looked inside. He never touched the worn leather of her handbag. He did not rape her, either. He possessed no carnal desires. In fact, his skin never touched hers. She didn't see the knife. Didn't see how it slid smoothly from beneath his coat. How it gleamed in the sun. How it moved, seeking her out. She never saw any of this. She only felt it. Felt each thrust of the knife as it slid into the giving soft of her belly. (I won't beleaguer the sexual connotations of a knife parting flesh, but you see my point.) As it sliced skin and muscle. As she was stabbed twenty-seven times.

The crowd came quickly. They seemed to materialize from the air.

Hundreds of people arrived as the blade made its first journey from sunlight to that warm soft place inside her. They stood as the blade created its own, new, vaginal opening in the girl, as the blade slide, penetrating her like some final lover. They watched with wide, vacuous eyes, milky eyes that glinted with strange far off joy. They watched her life being stolen and they did nothing to stop it. No one stepped forward. No one said "leave her alone." No one tackled this minor demon. No one ran for help. No one called for the police. No one helped.

They watched, and in some ancient reptile part of their brains, they enjoyed. Their hearts raced. Their respiration quickened. This was like pornography, dark, secret pornography. Like the whispered legend of the snuff film, but better. This was true. This was live. In Technicolor. In stereo. And just a few delicious feet away. This was what they had lived their sad, quietly desperate lives for. This was their moment. The one they would think about as they drifted off to sleep. The one they would whisper about at cocktail parties. The one they would tell their grandchildren about.

Finally. This was their dark secret.

As the young girl quietly melted into the cobblestones, and her assailant slowly walked away unencumbered, chased by no one, I watched the world end. I don't claim to be better than them. I stood and watched. I was part of the crowd. Though I would like to deny it, my reptile brain salivated with joy right along with the others. No, I am no better. But at least I understand the implications. I can see what we have come to. That day I watched a sun go Nova, and I have waited twenty-seven years for the blast wave to cross the cold miles and reduce all of us walking corpses to ash where we stand.

I think it may finally be here.

And I never even guessed what would bring it. I'm ready for it. But not quite yet. Give it time. Be patient. It will come.

This morning's newspaper tells of mounting tension in Pakistan. They have the bomb now. The big one. And it's not just great nations like the U.S., Russia, and China anymore. Everyone has a thermonuclear device. Small disorganized terrorist sects have suitcase bombs. Tribes in places that haven't mastered running water have an atom bomb or two. The pope has an ICBM. The edges are beginning to fray. The center will not hold.

Not just that. Not just yet. The strong force, nuclear fission could wipe the slate clean. It could erase us from history in an instant. All that we have built and accomplished could be un-built, un-accomplished. We could be unmade. What a shame that would be. We don't deserve the clean flash, the instant oblivion. We deserve much worse. Not a bang. A whimper. A long, slow, despondent whimper.

I hope they can hold off just a little longer. I hope they can wait. Please keep your finger off that button. The end we deserve is coming, and soon, I think. Soon.

Escape Velocity

I was blind. My blindness was self induced. I had built a wall around myself that was twenty-seven years thick, and I hid behind it. Like all the other monkeys I saw only the things I wanted to. I told myself that everything was fine. That the world wasn't falling apart, wasn't coming unglued around me. I lived in the sort of silent fear that has invaded modern life like a virus. Fear permeates our every thought, our every action. Sweat, and the coppery taste of adrenaline underlay everything we smell, everything we eat. It is the unremembered dream that shocks us awake at three a.m., it is the tension that holds us in place. It is the subtext of our days.

Drinking overly strong coffee in the morning, working my muscles to exhaustion at the gym, working in my dungeon cubicle, lying in bed with anonymous women; these acts, these overt actions serve only to paralyze my mind. To insulate my consciousness against the grim reality that God has gone mad. The world has slipped over the edge.

It all comes down to escape velocity. The speed necessary to get away from something. If you are on the planet Earth the escape velocity is six miles per second. A black hole is a collapsed star. Its mass is unimaginably huge, yet it exists in very little space. Infinite density. The gravitational field is so powerful that not even light can escape its pull. Nothing can resist its power. The planetary madness we have succumbed to is like a black hole.

As you approach it, the pull grows stronger. Space and time warp into an ever deepening curve toward it. You slide toward the Schwarzchild radius: the event horizon, the place where the escape velocity equals the speed of light. Here there is no turning back. Time slows, becomes meaningless. Density begins to increase. Madness. The terminus.

Let me tell you about the event horizon. The overt act I told you about. The overly strong coffee sending little billows of steam up from the Formica top of my kitchen table to caress my face tells me that it is morning. My eyes are bloodshot from too much gin and not enough vermouth. The night before is little more than a blur. A party. I think I had been at a party. My mind was filled with bits of mindless conversation, and loud music. I could remember drinking a massive number of martinis and later lying on a bed covered with coats and jackets and purses while a short blonde named Debbie very slowly, very expertly sucked my cock. Debbie. Or maybe Delores. Something like that.

I was playing that very enjoyable memory over as I scanned the paper. I was quietly humming "Pennies From Heaven". I hummed often. It was a way to block thought, and keep myself blind. My humming was, as always, meaningless.

I wouldn't even have known that song if I hadn't seen the Steve Martin movie. I had seen it on a date. She was Alicia. My date. I had met her at a Christmas party my firm had held. She was a receptionist. Or a secretary. I don't remember for certain. We had gone to see that Movie. She had expected goofy comedy, light entertainment. I had come without expectations. She hated the movie. I loved it. Afterwards we fucked. I never called her again. It had been a long time since I was on a real date.

The paper spoke of more dead in Ireland. More dead in Israel. More dead in Detroit. Fires somewhere out west. Floods in the south. Drought in the east. Same shit as every other day. Mounting tensions. Then, buried near the human-interest stories, almost as an afterthought I saw her. She was barely worth reporting, barely worth mentioning.

Maybe it was such a small story because she was such a small girl. Maggie. Maggie Swain. That was her name. Maggie was seven years old. Maggie would be seven years old forever. The picture showed her smiling. Her wide mouth displaying a gap where a tooth would never grow. The tooth fairy had wasted a quarter on that one.

Maggie had been playing in her back yard. She lived in a good neighborhood. She was surrounded by a tall chain-link fence. Her mother was just a few feet away, separated from the cheerful girl by a screen door. She was in what should have been the safest place in the world.

Then she was gone. Vanished. Another of the disappeared. The ghost children. It has become open season on children now. Just another sign of our disease. Children have become something to be used and discarded. Maggie was used and discarded. I could see her little face looking sadly up at me from the paper. I could imagine pleading in her eyes. Her photo winked at me. This wasn't real. None of this was real.

A fisherman found her broken doll body on the edge of the lake. Her baby flesh was naked, exposed to the elements. She had lain there, without clothes, without protection, without dignity, without love, for two days. She was dropped there a few short hours after going missing from her yard. Lured with candy or a shiny toy into a waiting car, she had been swept away forever. Used and discarded. She was raped and her throat cut before being dumped near the water. Fucked and thrown away. Just another disposable consumer item. We are all biodegradable.

Now she was one of the ghost children who haunt us. Another victim. We have all become victims. This world is very dark and filled with monsters with very sharp teeth. They feed on our children. The real horror of it is how easily we accept it. How little we notice it. A little girl stolen from her home, raped, murdered and thrown away like a broken doll was barely unusual enough to make the papers. It just couldn't compare to the mounting tensions heading us toward global extinction.

Little Maggie Swain was the event horizon. That's when I knew we had reached the point of no return. No turning back for us. No escape velocity. The line between light and dark, between the day side of the planet and the night side is known as the Terminator. The Terminator. The Terminus, the point where the trip ends. The last stop on the line. No trains past this point, my friend. No escape velocity.

Just Like The Girl

Here's what I decided to do. My grand reaction to all the horror around me was this: I would ignore it. No change at all, really. I would simply bury myself even deeper into my nihilistic lifestyle. Epicurus would be proud of how I deadened my mind and my heart to the gentle terrors of a mad world.

In short: if Rome was going to burn, I was going to fiddle. As I said, no change, really.

So here's what happened: Work and party. It was a diurnal system. I worked during the day, and partied at night. Sleep was not a priority. If I could just drink enough to push the terrors from my mind then I wouldn't have to worry about the ghost children, and the puddles of blood seeping through cobblestones that haunted my mind, and floated behind my eyelids. Liquor, loud music and increasingly anonymous sex with women I not only didn't love, but probably wasn't even attracted to , became the anesthesia that I used to numb myself.

I was like a shark. I had to keep moving. If I stopped to think, I ran the risk of waking up. Of really seeing the world. I was doing everything I could to kill my insight. To stop seeing at all. I would have succeeded if I hadn't met Walter. Wait. Not that. Not just yet. First I need to tell you this:

J.J. Astor made his fortune by selling animal skins to Indians. First he would sell the poor Redskins cheap liquor, but not too cheap. Then, when they were good and drunk, he'd sell them his overpriced furs and skins. Fleecing them with fleece, so to speak. He's one of our greatest heroes.

Now, Walter.

At first I thought he was just another shark; gliding through the late night Bacchanals like me, just another mindless hedonist living on cocaine and joyless blowjobs. I couldn't have been more wrong.

The house belonged to a middle-aged woman named Suzanne. She was one of those upper income hostesses who fought to remain young and hip. She was a whirl of collagen and silicone. A dervish of Prada, and Versace. She threw a constant party where the booze and the drugs were free. It was all

16

part of the price she paid to be loved. Wanted. Needed.

The place was huge. The marble floors had a reflective quality that made them seem transparent, as if they were a sheet of glass stretched over a bottomless abyss of legs and feet and crotches.

I was wandering the room, gripping a very cold gin and tonic and admiring the reflected feet below me. Chinese women used to bind their feet. They would wrap them tightly in silk, starting when they were children. Over the years this would permanently deform their feet, causing them to become stunted and misshapen. These strange bird feet were seen as highly attractive. Men would become sexually excited just thinking about those broken little feet.

In my culture a huge number of men find sexual excitement in sadism as well. They are turned on by broken faces covered in semen. By bound hands and gagged mouths.

Earlier I had been eyeing a skinny brunette. She was like one of those emaciated girls you see in Calvin Klein ads. Her hips were non-existent. Her breasts were a myth. I had been thinking that it would be an interesting experiment; seeing if fucking her made me feel queer. Then she left with an old man in a shark skin suit. I decided that it was just as well. I was probably too drunk to be any real danger to her anyway.

Now I was just wandering the room, absorbing the vibe and thinking about feet. Looking down and not where I was going was what caused me to meet Walter. I ran directly into him.

He was huge. So big that I had to crane my head back to see his face, which loomed above me like a transient moon. His eyes were deep set and dark. I couldn't tell if they were brown or black, but whatever color they were they had a piercing quality. A thick, brown beard that made him look like Grizzly Adams covered most of his face. There was something god-like to his stature. He was more statue than man.

As we collided, my gin and tonic upturned against his stomach, producing a dark patch on his blue shirt. My first feeling was fear. I had a simple understanding that this man could probably kill me with one swing of his massive fist.

Instead of raining destruction upon my face, he laughed. It was a booming, earth-shaking laugh that silenced the room. I couldn't help it. I started laughing with him. We laughed. He laughed like the Jolly Green Giant. I laughed like a lunatic spending his first night outside the asylum. We just kept laughing. The entire room had stopped to stare at the two nuts in the corner cackling insanely and that made us laugh even harder. Somewhere in all that laughter Walter and I became friends.

He wasn't a cubicle slave like me. Not Walter. He wasn't a nine to five kind of guy. Over the last fifteen years he had lived in twenty cities, and had more jobs than he could remember. He had been a longshoreman, a meat packer, a secretary, a waiter, a reporter, a movie stuntman, a shipping clerk, a semi-pro boxer, a construction worker, a baggage handler, a bouncer, a telemarketer, a bicycle messenger, a security guard, and a million other things. He told me this as we wove through the tightly packed, sweaty bodies that gyrated together with the mood of the room. We were making our way toward the bar to replace the drink I had emptied on his shirt and the one he had emptied into his mouth.

We had almost reached our objective when I spotted her. She was clearly quite vulnerable. Her eyes had that wide-open quality that suggested someone new to this world of depravity and predatory sexual behavior. She was just off the bus from Iowa, or Idaho or some other ridiculous place like that. Maybe she had just broken up with her boyfriend; he was her first love. They had been dating since high school, and had often talked of marriage. Now she was alone, a wounded bird in a room full of hawks. Sometimes I seem to know more than I should. I seem to sense these things about people. I could see it in those wide, brown eyes. Eyes that would succumb so easily to tears. Eyes that would stare longingly as she confessed every secret, every hope, every desire.

My first instinct was to abandon Walter and make my way to her. To offer a kind word and a strong drink. It would be simple to coax her into a quiet part of the house; to ply her with feigned kindness and liquor. My desire to abuse this soft little creature was strong, but my need for another drink was even stronger.

Walter saw me looking at her. I couldn't tell if he had been entertaining the same ideas I had, but I assumed his thoughts were at least similar to mine.

"Are we gonna get that drink, or what?" I asked. He nodded and we continued toward the bar.

The wounded bird's name was Pauline, but I wouldn't learn that for two more days.

The bar was crowded and we had to wait for our refreshments. We spent the time looking about the room: sizing up the people. They all had a sameness about them. It was as if they were completely interchangeable. I could never keep them straight; I would be approached by someone and find myself uncertain if this was the person that I had just spent fifteen minutes talking to, or someone I had never met before. It was as if they were all products spit out by some assembly line in some huge factory. They were just different models of the same product, with only the most superficial of differences.

This homogeny made things very confusing. It was a constant struggle to keep the night's memories organized, and the alcohol only made things worse. My mind had become a fog filled room. Ideas, thoughts, memories were merely vague shapes glimpsed momentarily through the moving mist. Now and then the fog would part, opening just wide enough for me to see the solid shape of reason. When this happened I would rush for another drink.

Finally, our drinks arrived. As he took the glass, Walter gripped the bartender's wrist. "Better get me another of these," he ordered then drained his glass in a single gulp.

I was gentler with my glass of gin and tonic. I nursed it. It survived for nearly two minutes, and left me wishing I had ordered a replacement when Walter ordered his. I looked longingly into the empty glass. A few lonely drops had welled at the bottom. I contemplated licking them out with my tongue and thought better of it. Instead, I stole the half-empty drink from the guy next to me. His head was turned and his attention was fully devoted to chatting up the Asian girl at the end of the bar. She wasn't paying any real attention to him.

"This party's dead. I know a better one 'cross town, you wanna go?" Walter was finishing another drink as he asked.

"Why not."

As we headed for the door, I spotted the wounded bird again. A gray haired Lothario with too much gold jewelry, and too much tanned skin was offering her a drink and a kind word. As we stepped through the door I saw him coaxing her toward a quiet part of the house.

The first monkeys shot into space died. Most people don't know that. The team at NASA planned every detail to perfection, but one. They simply forgot to provide an oxygen supply for those little apes. The mission was a resounding success. The rocket went up, just as planned. It orbited the Earth, just as planned. It came down, just as planned.

Everything was perfect. Except that when they opened the escape pod door they found two dead monkeys. Most people don't know that.

I can't remember riding in the car with Walter to the next party. I know that I must have, because we arrived together. Still, I remember watching that wounded little bird being led away by a greasy old man; then I remember walking through the door of a much louder party than the one we left.

These people were younger and better looking. They were somehow more alive, more vital. Maybe they just had better drugs and more booze. They absolutely hummed with excitement. Their young bodies vibrated with the music. Their heat was palpable. The room smelled of sex.

There were a hundred young girls willing and waiting. For some reason, though, I couldn't seem to stop thinking about that damn little bird. Pauline. But I didn't know her name yet. She was just the wounded bird. The innocent girl about to be taken advantage of. Probably already taken advantage of by then.

God I needed a drink.

Awake in Golgotha

I don't know when I left the party. It must have been morning. Somewhere along the way, I lost track of Walter. One minute he was there, the next he had vanished into the cigarette smoke and stale air.

I had been in the middle of a conversation. The same conversation I always had at parties. I, like everyone else, was preoccupied with the mounting tensions. I could talk for hours about nuclear winter, and enhanced yield warheads. What a word: *enhanced.* Somehow these warheads, these enhanced warheads, were better than the regular vanilla warheads. The old ones could only kill twenty billion people, but these new enhanced babies could kill fifty billion. At least they could, if there were fifty billion people to kill. Never mind that the Earth's population is only seven billion.

Neutron bombs, fission, fusion, mutation, fallout, radiation sickness, breeder reactors, the China Syndrome, meltdown. These were the things I discussed at parties. I cheerfully told people that when the bomb hit Hiroshima, people's shadows were burned into the ground. I told them that the children around Chernobyl would all be born with leukemia for the next sixty years. I told them that if a breeder reactor melts down, the core rods will burn all the way through the earth.

They looked at me funny.

When the industrial revolution first got fired up, a scientist named Nikoli Tesla was very worried. He believed that all the new machines would cause so much vibration that they would actually vibrate the earth to death. He thought that the planet would split in two. People looked at him funny, too. But he really wasn't that far off.

It does not take a great leap to see a direct line from those first simple machines to the mechanical heat that we seem so intent on raining down on ourselves.

I had been in the midst of telling all this to a young stockbroker when I noticed Walter was gone. I had turned to say: "you understand me, don't you?" when I saw that he wasn't there.

At first I was worried. I wondered what had happened. Then I decided that he must have followed some girl across the room. I thought that maybe I should do the same. I looked around and spotted a young woman on her own. She looked decidedly drunk.

Her eyes were half lidded, and she was breathing through an open mouth. Her skin was too pale. Despite all of this, she was clearly quite beautiful, just not currently at her best. She must have been about nineteen or twenty. She was slim, but not skinny. Her hair was a fiery red, and hung long around her shoulders. I couldn't see the color of her eyes from where I was standing, so I decided to get closer.

I was drunk enough to stumble as I walked toward her. I kept bumping into people. They were packed so tightly together that I had to squeeze my shoulders in just to navigate the room. The odor of sweat and cigarettes and something like old *pate* was thick, and for a moment I could feel the last several drinks trying to make their way back up my throat. I stopped for a second, and the feeling passed as quickly as it had come.

I saw a young man also making his way toward my prey, and I thought I might lose her to him. It became a sort of race. I was fighting to fit between the sardine people before he could get to her. He almost beat me, but he wasn't quick enough.

Standing over her, I felt very powerful. And much less drunk than I had a moment before. I can't remember what I said to her, but it worked. Soon she was leading me by the hand down a darkened hall. She opened the first door we came to. Inside a plump brunette was on her hands and knees. A skinny black man was fucking her from behind while she fellatted a boy who could not have been more than sixteen. His pimpled face had a look indistinguishable from agony. We watched for a second, then ventured further down the hall.

Some people confuse pleasure and pain. It's an easy mistake to make. In the end they do seem to be largely the same thing.

As she pushed me down onto the floor, I thought again of the wounded bird being led into the darkness. The sound of my fly being unzipped made me forget about her for the moment.

I awoke in late afternoon to find the previous evening a blur in my mind. I had only vague memories at first. I would see flashes of activity, here a face, there a bit of conversation. As I moved around the house performing the little routines that make the day, my memories began to gel; to solidify. I could remember almost everything that had happened. I found myself wondering about Walter and what had become of him.

For the moment I had no thought of the wounded bird.

Work. Or what passed for it. Safely enclosed in my cubicle I fought sleep and popped Excedrin every few minutes to combat the massive hangover that was forcing down on me like a thousand pound stone. The hours moved slowly, and despite not arriving at work until two o'clock it seemed that five would never arrive. I knew that I was in danger of being fired if I continued to miss so many mornings and leave early so many afternoons. I didn't care.

Evolution has worked for millions of years to create the perfect organism. Natural selection has weeded out the weak and the inferior so that only the best adapted survive and breed. The process is far from random. It has all been toward a specific end. Most seem to assume that man, with his 747 brain and opposable thumbs is that best of all possible beasts. They are wrong. Humans are merely a speed bump on the way to perfection. We are incubators. We serve as a testing ground for evolution's true goal: the virus. Natural selection created us as a means to build the perfect virus, and we have been good at our jobs. Just look at antibiotics. What better way to ensure better, stronger, more resilient viruses?

The morning's paper offered the wonderful tale of a man robbed in the street. After giving up his wallet and watch he was forced to the ground, stripped, castrated and left to bleed to death. Just another day in the petri dish. Welcome home.

Rent Control

After the industrial revolution really got into high gear, corporations began looking for ways to maximize profits. A factory or a mine would be built. Then the company would surround the factory with its own little city. The workers would rent houses that belonged to the company. They would buy everything they needed to live from the company store. Their children would attend the company school.

In this way the company was able to take back all of the wages it paid its employees. They didn't call this slavery. They called it free enterprise.

Days spent in my cubicle were broken up by lunch breaks. I would purchase sandwiches and coffee from the firm's cafeteria. Things haven't really changed all that much.

I drink too much. But then, who doesn't? Sexual addicts don't take any real pleasure from the sex act itself. They use sex as a replacement for love, or acceptance. They feel dead when they aren't fucking.

Some people burn themselves with cigarettes. I understand this impulse. In fact, I endorse it strongly. Everyone should get into self-destruction. It's a great hobby.

Enhanced Yield

Somehow I had known that I would see Walter again. I didn't have to wait long. He arrived on my doorstep shortly after I returned home from work. I didn't think to ask how he had known where I lived.

Walter had a problem. He had just lost his apartment. His apartment, he explained, wasn't really his to lose. A friend who worked in the building had given him the key to a vacant apartment and he had been living there rent-free in secret. The building's owner had discovered this when he showed up to give a tour to a prospective tenant. Imagine the look of shock and surprise on their faces when they stumbled across a two-hundred pound man lying on the kitchen floor, nude and surrounded by empty beer cans and vodka bottles.

Walter was equally surprised. He jumped to his feet screaming and brandishing a massive erection. He chased them from the apartment wailing like a banshee. Their screams joined his in an insane cacophony as they all spilled out into the hall.

Needless to say that the prospects had decided against living in a building with such lax security, and Walter was now homeless. This was nothing new. Walter had found himself without home many times. He had lived on the streets of Detroit for a month. He had slept in doorways in Houston. He had spent nights in the parks of Chicago. Walter was the kind of guy who survived in any environment. Adaptation is the key to survival.

He needed a place to crash, and assured me that it would only be for a few days. I don't know why I said yes. Maybe I just wanted someone to drink with, or maybe I was a bit lonely. Whatever the reason I suddenly had a roommate.

We easily fell into a routine, Walter and I. Nights belonged to the bottle. We drank together, in my house and in other people's homes as well as clubs and bars and cars and anywhere we could find a drink. During the day I went off to work, and he did whatever it was that he did. It was a mystery that I had no desire to solve.

Walter didn't read the papers. I, on the other hand, devoured them. I was increasingly obsessed with the silent, newsprint terrors offered up in neat rows and columns of twelve point type. I couldn't turn away from the grainy black and white photos of corpses and car wrecks and world leaders pretending to hold off ultimate destruction. The papers where my excuse to drink.

Walter didn't need an excuse.

It was from one of these papers that I learned the name of my wounded little bird. I had forgotten her by then. She was just another blurred memory shoved down into the recesses of my mind; the place I put all of the things I didn't want to deal with. That particular part of my brain had become quite crowded over the years.

There, printed on paper that would leave my fingertips ink-stained, was the little bird looking up at me with dead eyes. When her body was first discovered, naked and bound with duct tape, she didn't have a name. She was another Jane Doe. But finally the police had connected her dental records to a history, a past, a life, a name. Pauline Skorse. Pauline was the wounded bird's name. Not that it really mattered.

She had arrived, as I had guessed, on a bus just two weeks before her death. She had been raped, and suffocated. The article said that six other girls had been killed in the same way, their naked bodies bound with duct tape like Pauline, in the last three months. The police suspected that all seven killings were the work of the same man. They feared, the paper went on to say, that this was the work of a serial killer.

Ted Bundy was the first person to be called a serial killer. That doesn't mean he was the first person to fit that description; just the first to be given a name. Albert Fish was killing and eating little girls in the thirties, but no one knew what to call him. I suppose that we have always had human super-predators. But now we seem to more of them than ever before. There are, according to the FBI, at least sixty working serial killers in the U.S. We seem to be breeding these monsters faster than we can breed their victims. Like the virus, they seem about to overtake us. To replace us on the food chain.

I suppose I felt sadness over the death of Pauline. I had watched her with amorous interest just two nights before. I had watched her led away by the man whom I now believed was almost certainly her killer. I could see her face, her wide, sad eyes. I imagined that as she was taken from the room by him she had looked back, over her shoulder at me with a quiet look of pleading in those eyes. I knew it wasn't true, but I could see it happening. I could feel those eyes begging for help, for salvation. Had I only known. But then, if I had, would I have helped? I don't know. I don't want to know.

Walter didn't remember Pauline. I asked him, and he had no memory. He wasn't interested in the dead bird. He simply didn't care. When I told him that I had considered hitting on her, he laughed. He found it delicious. Oh, he said, how exquisite. He loved the irony. If only I could have slept with her before she was killed, what a story that would make. How beautiful.

After hearing his thoughts on the subject I poured us each a stiff scotch, and we started trying to decide where to go that night. Walter knew of a party that had been going for three days, but I wanted to check out a new club called *The Downward Spiral* .

After a few drinks we settled on the club. Walter preferred parties, where the drinks were invariably free, but I was paying so he was willing to accept my choice.

Somnabus

The electronic music was so loud that I feared it would interfere with the rhythm of my heart. The bass sounds seemed to vibrate my fillings, and make the bones of my joints clank together painfully. Add to this the incredible heat of so many bodies packed so closely together and the odor of sweat laced with high doses of liquor and I was in an exquisite sort of pain. I hated it immediately.

Walter was in heaven. The women outnumbered the men, three to one, which he saw as a perfect ratio.

We had to wait an interminable period for drinks. The bar was buried behind a throng of swaying young bodies. The four bartenders were much more interested in flirting with the girls than in filling drink orders. Those of us slowly dying of thirst just couldn't compete with the lure of single, attractive, mildly intoxicated women. I couldn't blame them; firm breasts did seem more important than pouring tequila for six-fifty an hour.

Finally Walter fought his way through the crowd and obtained our drinks. As we started working on our bourbon and cokes, we made our way across the room, eyeing the girls, trying to pick out two from the herd.

The women in these sort of places always seem to move in groups of three or more. Perhaps it comes from some sort of safety instinct, some genetic memory. The herd instinct is strong. Predators have little chance against a group packed tightly together with the weaker members hidden in the center. Whatever the cause, it was maddening. Our attempts at companionship would be greatly hampered by these tight little groups. We decided to redouble our efforts and press on.

The music had succeeded in giving me a horrible headache, and the difficulty that would be involved in getting another drink was hardly worth the effort. I was entertaining thoughts of giving up and drinking at home when Walter pointed them out. They were standing in the corner, laughing at some joke that had passed between the two of them. They both held drinks: not slushy girly drinks, but what seemed to be straight scotch, or maybe bourbon. These young ladies were real drinkers, a fact we saw as a good omen.

They were young; probably in college. They were slender and nicely constructed. Not beautiful, but very pretty. Looking at them I imagined that their flesh would smell of some perfumed soap from a specialty shop and perhaps lotion; it would be a clean, youthful smell. Their cigarettes made the Freudian in me think of oral fixations; this thought brought a faint smile to my face. I don't smile convincingly. People look at me funny when I smile.

I wondered, for a moment, why they were alone. Why weren't these two beauties, these sylphs surrounded by young men offering drinks, asking them to dance, asking for their numbers? These thoughts gave me a bad feeling. Maybe they were somehow unapproachable; lesbians or feminists or just angry.

I pushed these thoughts away, drained my drink, and followed Walter toward them.

We had to push between the tightly packed revelers. Luckily Walter went first and used his massive size to clear a path for me to follow.

The sheer density of the noise meant that we had to shout just to be heard. Walter did the talking. I just stood by and tried to smile charmingly. I told you, I don't smile well. I look crazy when I try, like a maniac attempting to wear a mask of sanity; a mask that has slipped slightly revealing the monster beneath, with its wild eyes and off kilter cracked grin. My smile makes people nervous.

Slippage

Looking in the mirror I noticed the scratch on my face. It started next to my left eye, and curved down under my jaw. I couldn't remember how I had gotten it. I couldn't remember much of the previous evening. At some point we had wandered into a convenience store. The buzzing, shifting, clicking light from the fluorescent tubes had made me feel woozy. If I hadn't needed cigarettes, I would have rushed back out the door.

Standing in line for my turn to bargain for the overpriced necessities of life, I watched the gray old man in front of me struggle with a handful of change. He just wanted a lottery ticket, but the old, scarred coins wouldn't cooperate with him.

His hand must have trembled, because the handful of change cascaded out of his grasp. Some coins came to rest on the counter, others spun and rolled in slow, wobbly arcs before collapsing on their sides. Still others made way for the floor. The old man tried a shaky grin at the clerk and said: "Every time it rains..."

The round, dark clerk scooped coins from the counter and finished: "Pennies from heaven".

My head ached and I had vomited once already, but I was determined to be in my cubicle by nine. As much as I hated it, I needed this job.

Walter and I had stumbled in around four. No. That was wrong. I had stumbled in around four; Walter hadn't been with me. I wasn't certain when we had parted company, but I had definitely come home alone.

On my left palm I noticed a smear of what looked like blood. I assumed it was from the rather nasty scratch of my face and washed it off. Shaving was a problem. There was no way I could do a competent job of it without ripping open my wound and probably ruining my shirt in the process. I decided to skip it.

I brushed my teeth and tried to brace myself for the rest of the day.

Most people think Thomas Edison invented the light bulb. He did not. It was actually invented by a man named Joseph Swan. Edison and Swan went into business together, and made a killing selling electric lights, tinted red, to the owners of run down, filthy, disease ridden whore houses in the worst corners of New York's tenderloin district. Edison and Swan knew precisely who their clientele were.

Henry Ford ruled his employees with an iron fist. He would send investigators to make surprise inspections of their homes. He demanded that their surroundings be clean and neat, that they abstain from alcohol and smoking, that they speak only English, and that they attend church. If any rule was transgressed they would be summarily discharged.

Thomas Jefferson, the second chief executive of the United States owned slaves. He even impregnated a young slave girl whom, we can guess, he took to his bed by force. He refused to acknowledge the fruit of his union with this poor girl, and the child grew to adulthood in slavery.

These men are our heroes. History is written by the winners and teaches a very strong lesson: it doesn't matter what evil men do, as long as those men prevail. History reflects the point of view of those who sculpted it. In time it becomes stone, lapidary words carved on vellum; gestalt.

The question is: which men, if any, will prevail in this strange time? In this world of mounting tensions, of possible *humanacide*, of children hunted like beasts of the field, how can anyone survive?

I thought about these things as I busied myself with coffee and the morning paper and cigarettes. The cigarettes were a relatively new habit. Walter was sleeping on the couch. I don't know when he came home, but as usual he had managed to find his way back to my couch before I awoke.

The paper offered a fresh horror. In its pages I learned that... Not yet. I'm not ready to tell that yet. I need more time to explain. You see, this isn't just my story, its Walter's too, and more than being our story it's a warning, and perhaps a bit of a confession. So, before I can burden you with what I found in that newspaper I have to try to make you understand. For Walter's sake.

While in Mexico, whacked out of his mind on a startling variety of drugs, the novelist William S. Burroughs shot his wife in the head, killing her, while playing William Tell with a .38 and a high ball glass. It was an accident, but that didn't make her any less dead.

When I tell people these things they look at me funny. Samuel Johnson once said: "You mustn't mind me, madam. I say strange things, but I mean no harm". I wonder how much harm I have meant. The world is crumbling around us. It is doing its best to careen into oblivion and we are helping in every way we can. We are all formulated for death, hard wired for self destruction. And many of us are designed for the destruction of others. Nature or nurture, who gives a fuck? Maybe Walter's mother beat him, or the local priest raped him three times a week, in the end does any of that matter? Is it any sort of surprise that as the world has gone mad, madness has become a way of life? Of course we are breeding maniacs and predators. We're not just breeding them; we're training them. We are becoming. Mutation, adaptation, survival. We all adapt to fit our environment. We must. Adaptation equals survival. Mutation is the only smart bet.

At heart we are all killers. Some are just more comfortable with it than others. Hell some are down right at home with homicide. That morning I began to suspect that I was living with someone who was very comfortable with death.

Walter, sleeping deeply on my couch, curled among the myriad stains and cigarette burns, dreaming whatever madness his mind cultivated in the quiet of sleep, suddenly frightened me more than I could have imagined just a few minutes earlier. I was filled with the belief that at any moment he would spring from sleep and kill me in a variety of ways.

Let me tell you why I believed this. The paper, like every morning's paper, was filled with the gentle terrors that made up daily existence here on the edge of the empire. Page one had more about the growing tensions with China. By the third page I had learned all I wanted to know about a young woman who had submersed her four-month old son in boiling water because he cried all night. Murder, rape, assault, child molestation, mounting terror, madness, it was the same as any other day. Nothing special.

Then I saw something that made my fingers tighten around the edge of my paper, the muscles contracting until the newsprint began to tear slightly from the force. I began to shake softly.

There was a long article about the most recent victim of a suspected serial killer. The man who had used and discarded the wounded bird, Pauline, had struck again. And again I recognized the victim. I recognized her from the bar. She had been talking with a friend when Walter and I approached them. Walter had hit it off with the dead girl. I had beaten him home. All other details had been stolen by liquor and sleep deprivation.

It suddenly seemed vital that I remember exactly what had occurred last night. I thought that I had left with one girl, Walter with the other. And now Walter's date was dead. He must have taken her to some dark, secret place and done unspeakable things. He must have devoured her. But why? How?

I had seen Walter as another me; just another disillusioned bastard, beaten down by the madness of the world, doing his best to paralyze his mind, to fight down his empathy, to live a perfect life of quiet, desperate apathy. Now I realized that I couldn't have been more wrong. Walter had decided to fight back in the most extreme way he could: he had decided to quit being apathetic, to fuck being part of the solution, he had chosen to be the problem, to be the disease, the madness of the universe. As I have said before: I don't smile convincingly.

I feared him, but somehow I admired his extreme measures.

Take any rigid surface and hit it. Hit it again. Hit it enough times, with enough force and slowly stress fractures begin to form. Minute cracks crawl across it like delicate spider webs. The cracks grow, connecting, widening until the integrity of the structure is breached and total collapse occurs. Things fall apart.

The human mind is like this. When the whole world is insane maybe the only defense against it is to join the ranks of the mad. Part of me longed to throw off the strait jacket of humanity, to refuse to sing in my chains like the sea, to take up arms against the universe. I could see my self as a postmodern Alexander, standing over the Gordian knot and snarling "fuck it" as I sliced through the warm, soft tissue of some innocent human body. Madness, wrap your dark wings around me.

But even so, some part of me that was still human rebelled. Something inside me that the world had been unable to batter into submission cried out to hold on to whatever it is that makes us human, even if most of us were not fully human anymore.

Now I had to decide what to do about the sleeping killer on my couch. I wrestled with this for awhile, then decided the best solution was to take him out drinking. Tonight we would find a loud place filled with beautiful people and we would drown ourselves in liquor of every variety. We would drink until all rational thought had been extinguished. We would drink until the entire world simply floated away on a sea of booze. It would be just like every other night.

I thought for a bit and decided that what I needed immediately was a very long, very hot shower to clear my mind and get my muscles in full working order. Work, which just a few minutes earlier had seemed a necessity, had vanished from my mind like some obscure date barely memorized in a high school history class. It was just not applicable to my real existence. I walked, shakily, to the sink and drew a large glass of water, tried not to think about the chemicals that had run off from the waste of a pharmaceutical company and seeped slowly through the soft, arable soil, finally coming to rest in the ground water supply and beginning the long trip through pipes, and filters, a reservoirs to come pouring out my kitchen tap like liquid death. I tried not to think of the well evolved, antibiotic immune bacteria that had grown strong feeding off the waste products of what passes for normal human intercourse these days and migrated to the crystal water reserves. I tried not to think of the alien micro organisms that were surely swimming about in the cool, clean looking void of my water glass, and I drank.

It seemed imperative that I not wake Walter, not just yet. So I moved slowly, quietly toward the bathroom. I adjusted the water temperature until it was perfect for boiling lobsters, then I climbed in. My flesh revolted against the stinging heat. I nearly yelped, but fought it back. I closed my eyes as the water cascaded over me like boiling oil.

The steam rapidly filled the enclosed space. It grew so thick that breathing became difficult, like breathing underwater. My lungs had to work at twice their normal force to merely fill and empty their space and refill it again.

When I was younger, just a little kid, sometimes I thought I was something else. I had these dreams that I wasn't a human at all. I was an alien. One of the alligator people, from the alligator planet. I was just wearing this human skin until the other alligator people came back to get me. Even then, I knew I was different. There is no empathy among the alligators.

I scrubbed my skin with a forcefulness that was somehow unnatural. I scrubbed and abraded my skin until it was raw and inflamed. I scrubbed as if I could some how wash away memory, wash away understanding, wash away reason and logic. It was to no avail. I was beyond cleanliness, yet I still knew and understood all that I had upon entering the shower.

My legs began to feel weak. My muscles seemed on the verge of abandoning me. I collapsed into a heap on the floor of the shower, my body contracting into a fetal ball. And there, with the scalding water pummeling me skin, and the thick, hot steam clogging my lungs I began to do something that I hadn't done since childhood: I began, silently, to weep. These were not alligator tears. Oh, Walter, my apathy is every bit as insidious as your evil.

Slowly the water that rained down on me began to cool, and eventually to run cold. After the extreme heat the cold was unbearable, yet I remained. I lie there, naked, cold, shivering and alone for nearly an hour. Then I forced myself to rise, stop the flow of water and climb from the shower.

As I dried and dressed myself I could hear the sounds of Walter coming through the door. He would be smoking the day's first cigarette, possibly fixing himself a small morning bracer, and rummaging through the icebox in search of whatever would pass for breakfast this morning. Walter would eat anything. He was like some huge, ambulatory garbage disposal. Anything even vaguely edible went between his massive, gnashing jaws.

Temptation

Albert Einstein urged President Roosevelt to push for the development of an atomic bomb. He felt that it was imperative that the U.S. complete this mission before the Germans. Despite what Einstein believed, the Germans were never really close to building their own A-bomb. Years later Einstein would say that his urgings had been a mistake, that all of his research, his theories which led to that greatest of discoveries, the splitting of the atom, had been folly. If he had only known that the Germans would fail to create their own world killer, he would not have taken part in America's quest. Hindsight is, as the rubric goes, twenty-twenty.

I should never have taken that shower. I should have killed Walter while he slept. While, I would come to understand, I slept as well. It was too late for that, and in the long run I suppose there were very definite, very forceful parts of me that wanted Walter around, that didn't care if he was some inhuman creature, that in fact liked the thought of his cruelty. So I was just going to have to deal with it.

Standing behind the safety of the closed bathroom door I considered my choices. I could go out and act as if I simply didn't know what he had been up to each night while I was passed out cold. Or I could stand in front of him and shout *j'acuse!*, I know you, I know what you've done! Or I could simply wait there in the solitude of the toilet until the world passed away into the void of oblivion that was certainly rushing up to devour us all.

None of these choices seemed particularly appetizing. Finally I decided that the most sensible choice, the safest choice, was to go on, for now, as if nothing had changed. So I sauntered out and called hello to my serial killer room mate.

He was standing, like a mountain, in the kitchen. He held a bottle of Budweiser in one massive hand, and a box of Twinkies in the other. He was clad only in a threadbare pair of boxer shorts and a single sock. His hair was disheveled, and flattened on one side. There were deep, red lines on his cheek where the sheet that served as his only blanket on the couch had cut into his skin as he slept the sleep of the pure and untroubled.

"Morning," he grumbled, "Want some?" He held out the Twinkies toward me. I couldn't imagine eating; not now, maybe not ever, not with the pictures that my mind insisted on piling upon me. I shook my head and walked past him toward the sink. I could feel his eyes on my back as I ran another glass of water.

I was suddenly gripped with an intense desire to tell him everything I knew. To confess what I had learned and what I suspected. Why, I wondered. What would that accomplish? To what end was the madness aimed? And if I did, what then? Did I think that I could somehow convince him to change, to stop, to turn himself in? Or did I want to join him? I didn't know then, and I still don't.

I closed my eyes for a moment and saw Pauline, the wounded bird. This time the wounds were real. The blood was real. Her body was broken, and I could see hands gripping her, holding her down. I could see her hands flailing, fighting, resisting. My own hand went reflexively to my face to touch the mysterious scratch there.

"Walter, " I said without turning to face him, "when did you get home last night?" I didn't expect an answer, at least not an honest one. I expected him to ignore the question. He didn't.

"About four. Same as you." And with that he wandered out of the room. He never was much for conversation in the morning, so I wasn't surprised that he didn't feel like talking. His reply, however, left me a bit confused. I supposed that he was simply lying, counting on the ravages of alcohol to dull my recollections of the previous evening. I knew with certainty that I had beaten Walter home, and had been well asleep when he stumbled in. So, he had lied. Simple. The man was an amoral killer, a slaughterer of innocents, a rapist, a monster, so why should I be surprised that he was also a liar?

I realized that I had been gripping my water glass very tightly, so tightly that it had shattered without me noticing the razor edges slicing into the flesh of my palm, sending rivulets of bright, cheery blood running down my arm and dripping into a puddle at my feet.

Monkeys can learn to use American Sign Language to speak. With hours of arduous training they become quite proficient at communicating exactly what they need, what they want, what they hope for. They are, in their communication, very human. This fact makes it difficult for us to see them as just animals. Suddenly they seem so like us. Suddenly it seems wrong to torture them in experiments. Suddenly it seems wrong to cage them. Perhaps what we should learn from these talking monkeys is that the ability to communicate and build hospitals doesn't necessarily make us so special. Why do we assume that just because Plato, Chaucer, and Picasso were human that we are all superior to the monkeys? Rats aren't very smart. But then, they haven't built any atomic bombs. Cockroaches are far from anyone's idea of brilliant creatures, yet they rarely force each other into death camps.

I went to work cleaning the blood off my hand, and then wiped up the puddle from the floor.

Blood tastes like copper, but sweet. The higher your glucose level, the sweeter your blood will taste. I began to wonder why I knew that, and why I was thinking about it at that particular moment. A human can ingest quite a large quantity of blood with little ill effect.

When someone kills themselves by jumping from a tall building, they will first remove their glasses, assuming they wear glasses. It's a fact, many policemen have arrived at the scene of a jumper suicide to find an unbroken pair of glasses nestled safely on the ledge. We're conditioned to act a certain way, to do certain things, to behave within a set of limitations and rules. Sometimes I wonder what would happen if we refused to obey our conditioning.

I guessed that Walter had done just that.

Pro Se

I watch television. Television and television. Seeing at a distance. Television is the great ruiner of minds; the coma box; the glass teat. Karl Marx once said that religion is the opiate of the masses. He only said that because television hadn't been invented yet.

I've logged thousands of hours behind the cathode ray tube. The TV radiation has ruined my eyes, and my mind. I am constantly inundated by mindless sitcoms like *Doogie Howser, Friends,* and *A Family Affair.* I have drowned in a sea of schmaltz and smarm. I have been ruined for reality.

But sometimes reality encroaches upon the TV world. Not the *Dateline, 20/20,* handled, spun, focus group tested, marketing department approved reality; the real thing.

They used to call it station identification. Now it's just the commercial break. Just a few minutes for some multi-national corporation to bombard already weakened minds with the command to buy, to spend, to consume, to exercise your duty as a citizen. We have become a world of corporations where national boundaries and borders are meaningless.

But sometimes the ads aren't about shopping. Sometimes they have nothing to do with the drive to spend. Sometimes it's a plea to give. Sometimes it's an ad for a rape crisis center for children. A safe place for children who have been used: fucked and tossed away. Reality bleeds in.

It didn't have to be like this. We chose it. We worked toward it. According to the FBI there have been serial killers in the U.S. since the 1880's, but since 1975 the number has been growing rapidly; escalating at an exponential rate. We breed monsters faster than any other country. We need to. We are hardwired for destruction, formulated for ruin. This is what we have worked for. This is the point of all that mindless, dirty evolution. This is why we exist. Nature or nurture. Genetics forces the killer urge upon us. Our conditioning heightens it. Our parents make us the monsters we will become. We are the glorious disease.

I had come to a horrible decision, and a terrible conclusion. Finally I knew what I needed. Eight minutes from nova to burn. Twenty-seven years had suddenly collapsed around me into a single second. A singularity. A point of infinite mass. Infinite density. The event horizon. The terminus.

I wanted the heat of absolute destruction. For that I would need to talk to Walter.

Blowback

When a bullet enters a human body the force causes blood and tissue to be expelled in the opposite direction as the bullet's path. They call this blowback.

The conversation I had with Walter in my living room is little more than a blur in my mind. Details have evaporated. Only one thing really stands out: Pauline, the wounded bird.

Here is what happened: I confronted Walter. I told him everything I suspected. He didn't deny it. He stood there like a mountain and stared with his icy eyes until I thought they would corrode right through my skull and dissolve my brain.

Then I hit him with something huge. Something I could barely comprehend, but knew I needed to say. I told him that I wanted in on his game. I wanted to be his partner in depravity. I wanted to kill with him.

Walter's blank stare startled me. I had expected to die. To be pulverized by his massive hands. To be rent and broken. But if his look of confusion startled, his words shocked. Like freezing water poured on bare flesh, I felt the oxygen sucked from my lungs. I felt my heart cease to work, then sputter back to a start.

Blowback.

What he said was this: "You already have".

Blowback.

A very small spark ignites tightly packed gun powder, creating a rapidly burning fire. This fire superheats gasses, which then expand forcing a small lead projectile to move rapidly forward. Rifling on the inside of the gun's barrel causes the lead to spin. This little soft piece of lead will be moving at nearly the speed of sound as it leaves the gun, and passes through the air. As the bullet impacts with skin it punctures the flesh. Because the lead is so soft, it begins to deform. It mushrooms. Becoming flatter, and bigger around. It tears skin and muscle. If it hits a bone it will ricochet, changing direction within the body. The bullet leaves a channel of dead flesh behind it. As it passes out the other side of the body, it is so deformed and pushing so much tissue with it, that it leaves a much bigger hole than the one it entered through.

If you survive the trauma, and the ensuing shock, infection will kill you.

That canal of necrotic tissue will fill with bile, blood, and bacteria. This is sepsis. Death waits, but only a while.

Blowback.

Then he began to tell me about Pauline.

I had chosen not to remember. I had, somehow, simply turned off that part of my mind that records life for later viewing. I had locked so much of my existence away in a vault that I didn't posses the key to. Now it came, not in a rush of wavering flashback images from a forties b-movie, but in a little trickle, like a stream of water winding its way down a hillside to deposit itself against a rock where it will slowly build: first from a trickle to a puddle, then into a deep pond.

How deliciously I had tortured that wounded little bird. I could see her blood stained limbs flailing about in a ragged attempt to stem the force of my blows. I had killed her. Walter had held her in place so that she wouldn't be able to escape from the violence I rained down upon her. That I knew for certain. That, and that alone.

Why, was a question I couldn't answer. Sometimes there is no why. Earthquakes wipe out villages, buildings explode, and rain down upon pedestrians and passers by, disease wipes out hundreds of children, men drive cars through crowded playgrounds, lone gunmen take aim from bell towers. There is no why.

Somewhere, far back in my mind I looked for reasons. What had happened to me? What had made me like this?

The answer came. Nothing. Nothing was the answer. Nothing happened to me. *I* happened. I happened to the world. Me, and the others like me just were. We were our own creations. We were the next logical step in the evolutionary process. We are what's next.

Eventually the virus will rule. Until then, the world belongs to us. We are the top of the food chain. Albert Fish, Leonard Desalvo, Ted Bundy, John Wayne Gacy, Jeffrey Dahmer, David Berkowitz, Henry Lee Lucas, Walter and Me. We are the new Gods. Fuck the meek. We have inherited the earth.

So, here's what happened next.

Insects have yellow blood. It looks like pus; thick and gooey, and yellow. Lobsters' blood is blue. Real blue. Not like the mythical blue blood of aristocrats. Lobster blood is cool, azure. Humans, on the other hand, bleed red. So many wonderful shades of red. Bright, Halloween, movie red from capillaries in the surface of the skin. Dark, blackish red from the oxygen rich blood of arteries. We have nearly every shade of red in us. Walter and I set out to spill them all.

I never slept much, but now I was beginning a new phase of sleep deprivation. Walter and I would spend days awake. I quickly learned the very distinct levels of deprivation.

First comes *tired*. When you haven't slept much, you feel sleepy, and it's hard to keep your eyes open. Second is *exhaustion*. When you're exhausted not only is it hard to stay awake, but your body begins to ache. Your muscles feel as if they've been worked to their limits, and beyond. At this point it becomes difficult to think clearly. Your head starts to feel like its been filled with axle grease. At this stage I developed a permanent sniffle. The third stage is *breakdown*. Here there be tigers, my friend. Somewhere around eighty hours into wakefulness mild hallucinations begin. The pain moves from your muscles and into your bones, which feel like they've been fractured in thousands of places. A dull thud fills your brain, driving away thought. This is when you begin to notice your strange ideation. The final stage, more definite than anything in Kubler-Ross, is *oblivion*. Now all rational thought is gone. It is as if you've crashed through a wall, and sleep no longer seems necessary, or even desirable.

Walter didn't seem to feel any of the effects that plagued me. He was, to all appearances, invulnerable. He stood against pain like some great beast carved of marble, or granite. He grinned madly at agony.

Walter was, as far as I could tell, a god. He was some new sort of deity, built of pain. He was death, and pestilence, and suffering, and destruction, and plague.

Mr. Overby Has Fallen

This is the part where time starts to get fully out of whack. I've never been any good at keeping events in any sort of coherent order in my mind, but the memories I want to relate next seem to have no context, whatsoever.

There are three memories, three events that I know must have been separated by days, if not by weeks. Yet in my mind they seem to be simultaneous. I can find no way to untwist them from the single, tightly woven patchwork my brain has made. So I will tell these events as I perceive them.

In the kitchen, standing before the sink, scrubbing partially congealed blood from my hands and thinking about my shoes. My old tennis shoes are a mess. Covered in blood, which will never wash out, they are sure to have left recognizable imprints in the soft ground outside her window. They could be identified, they could lead back to me.

This was the first time I had thought in these terms. Walter was singing, loudly and badly out of tune. As he poured himself a drink he slaughtered the melody of *Pennies from Heaven*. His choice of song seemed oddly out of character, but I gave it little thought. I hit her again, as Walter grinned maniacally. Droplets of blood splattered across his face, some of it standing in stark relief against his too white teeth. We had crawled through the open window, and Walter had started the work of tying her up while she still slept, deep within her drunken fog. Walter pulled the knife from his boot and finished pouring his drink. The ice cubes clinked sadly as he lifted the glass to his lips.

She was starting to wake up, so I hit her with the flat edge of my hand. The blow connected with her mouth, splitting both her lips, and loosing a scream that must have been lodged in her throat. Walter reached around me for the soap, and began to scrub his hands merrily.

Walter had gone, and I was alone with her. He was somewhere in the house, but at that particular moment I didn't care where he was, or what he was doing. I was burning my shoes in a barrel behind my house. They had set in my closet for days, but they were never far from my mind. Once the idea of evidence occurred to me, I couldn't shake it. The shoes had to go. It didn't occur to my crazed mind that I had left fingerprints, hair, blood, saliva, semen, and numerous other traces at dozens of crime scenes. I never even thought of them as crime scenes. She was begging me not to kill her.

She had money, I could take it. She wouldn't tell. No one would ever know I had been here. She just wanted to live. No part of me felt sympathy for her. I knew from experience that although she was begging to live, soon she would be begging to die. I had barely started to work on her.

They used to put coins on the eyes of the dead. This tradition served a functional purpose. Before the advent of modern embalming techniques, and funeral preparation, it wasn't unheard of for the corpse to suddenly open their eyes at the funeral. Imagine how the grief stricken mourners must have reacted to this. The weight of the coins would hold the eyes shut. Like so many functional actions, myth was created to explain the use of these coins. They were, people said, to be used to pay the ferryman who would carry the departed across the river Styx, and into the afterlife. If the unfortunate was unable to pay, they would be forced to wander the earth for eternity, never able to rest.

I used Walter's knife to cut along the seam of her underpants. Her eyes were huge, and glossed over with panic. She has stopped using words, and now made only guttural, animal noises. I punched her hard in the stomach, and her breath flew from her in a massive rush. She coughed and choked.

The smoke from the barrel was black and acrid. It made it hard to breath, but I had to remain nearby, until the shoes were completely devoured by the greedy flames.

When Walter and I had both finished with her, I gutted her, and strung her intestines around the bed in loops. Walter refused to burn his shoes.

They used to put coins on the eyes of the dead. No one would put coins on this poor girls eyes, even if she had still had eyes. Her small, broken face looked up at me, black holes where her eyes had been, accusing me.

Walter finally had the blood washed from his hands. I was sitting at the table, a cup of coffee untouched in front of me, scanning the morning paper. New day, same news. I didn't read the stories that involved Walter and me. I didn't need to. And yet, I remained obsessed with the other news, the world events. Mounting tensions. Obsessed, yet uncaring. It no longer mattered if the whole human race committed suicide. The entire species could snuff itself, I wouldn't even notice.

Walter was lying on the couch reading *Popular Mechanics*, and sipping a glass of Jim Beam. I had begun to wonder when the police would knock at the door. when we would be led down some dark corridor, into a windowless room, inhabited by a small table, and grizzled police. When we would do our time under the hot lights.

They would beat us. I was certain of that. They would pile up mounds of evidence, circumstance, forensics, witnesses, statements, affidavits, and facts. They would crush us under the weight of their proof. And eventually, we would each be strapped to a padded table, arms outstretched like a crucifixion, and a needle would end our lives. State sponsored pest control.

Walter wouldn't worry about such things. Death was inevitable, he said. We should know that better than anyone. When they came for us, it would be humane, and clean, and quick. Those we came for were never so lucky. Pauline hadn't been so lucky.

I lit a cigarette. I took a slow gulp of my coffee. I looked at my hands. Very quietly, almost imperceptibly, I began to weep. For just a moment, one fleeting instant, I felt human. I felt guilt. I felt pity for anyone whose path I had crossed. I shook it off, and returned to reading my paper.

Walter

When I was young, there was a Juniper tree outside our house. I would sit under it, sheltered by the shade, and nap into the warm summer afternoon. My father cut it down one day. I hated him for it. I didn't see it as removal of wood, but as the murder of a living thing.

I loved that tree. Some cultures have worshiped trees. It's easy to understand why. They are so grand, so strong, so *permanent*. I dreamed of taking revenge on my father for killing my tree. In my mind I could see myself towering over him as he cowered on the ground where it had stood. I would drive long splinters of wood slowly into his eyes. They would puncture the soft sacks, releasing thick, pus like fluid which would trickle down his cheeks.

I never did that. Eventually I wasn't mad anymore. After all, it was just a tree.

Walter was pacing. Something was bothering him, but I had no idea what it was. He had been pacing since he came home, nearly an hour earlier. I didn't know where he had been, or what he had been up to. It was very unusual to see Walter this nervous. Normally nothing phased him.

He was absentmindedly rubbing his chin with one hand. I kept thinking that the three-day growth of stubble had to be abrading the flesh of his hand. Just thinking about it made my hand hurt. I began to work my thumb against my palm. He was starting to get on my nerves.

Walter's mood was catching. I had already been beginning to obsess about the possibility of being caught, but I had taken solace in the fact that Walter remained unconcerned. This new turn of events was simply too much to bear.

Cats eat mice. But more than just eat them, they toy with them first. The cat will cripple its prey, then allow it to escape, only to be caught again. The cat, once certain of victory, will repeat this process again, and again. The mouse will, eventually, become paralyzed by fear, unable to resist. When this happens, the cat grows bored, and has his meal.

No one thinks poorly of the cat for this cruelty. It is merely his nature.

There is an old story. I've heard it many times. I don't know where it originated. It goes like this:

One day an old woman was gathering firewood. She came upon a group of children tormenting a snake. They were stabbing it with sticks, and throwing stones at it.

Now the old woman couldn't stand to see any creature in pain. She drove the children away with harsh words, and scooped up the injured snake. She carried it home with her, and bandaged its wounds.

The old woman fed the snake, and nursed it to health. She cared for it, and in time she came to love it, and think of it as a pet.

One day, when the old woman was leaning over to serve the serpent its dinner, it struck and buried its fangs deep within the soft flesh of her hand. Venom began to coarse through her veins. As she lay dying the old woman asked the snake why it would do this to her. After all, she had rescued it, nursed it, fed it, loved it.

"Listen, lady," said the snake, "you knew I was a snake when you brought me home." We can't change our nature. We must embrace it.

Walter wouldn't tell me what was wrong. I tried several times to find out, but he stood mute. The way I knew he would if we ever went to trial. Walter would never talk, never break, never give in. It just wasn't in his nature. After awhile I gave up, and went to sleep. My dreams were fevered, and fitful.

I kept waking to the sensation of being watched. I would sit bolt upright in bed, and scan the dark room with my eyes. I would think, for an instant, that I had perceived some slight movement with the shadows. Then the sensation would fade, and I would realize that it had been nothing more than my imagination. I would settle back to the dream world, again.

In the dream I was tied. My hands were bound behind my body, and no matter how I struggled, I could not free myself. Walter was standing over me, laughing. His face and hands were smeared with blood. It wasn't my blood, I knew that for certain.

As I watched Walter, I saw myself walk from the shadows, and stand beside him. I was laughing, too. Not the me that was tied, but the other me, the one that stood by Walter. I knew then that they (we) were going to kill me. That I would be tortured, and murdered by them (us).

Then I awoke again. A thin sheen of sweat coated my body. Sleep, it seemed, would have to wait.

I climbed from bed, and made my way toward the kitchen. As I passed the living room I saw Walter sleeping on the couch. He was stretched out, limbs flung in every direction, deep within the confines of safe sleep. He slept the sleep of the just. He wasn't plagued with the nightmares that I had endured. Given his mood earlier, I would have assumed that he would find sleep as tenebrous as I had. Yet, here he was, sleeping like a baby.

In the kitchen I poured my drink, and began looking over the stack of old papers that sat on the table.

I began looking for stories that involved our exploits. I had made a point of not reading them. I hadn't even looked for them. I needn't have bothered.

I couldn't have read them if I had wanted to. I couldn't find them. They simply weren't there. Not a single mention of the dozens of murders Walter and I had committed. Except Pauline. The wounded bird. The first to die, and the last to rate a mention in the press. Only Pauline. Our victims had no obituaries. There were no stories about police trying to solve the mystery of young women tortured, raped, murdered, disfigured, disemboweled, eaten.

I found the article about the poor, wounded, dead little bird. Right there. It said that she was one of a string of victims, all belonging to the same man. Or so the cops surmised. But then, nothing.

The latest in a string of victims. But wasn't she the first?

It was as if none of it had ever happened. I couldn't figure out why. I knew that it had all been real. It wasn't that I was certain of my own sanity; in fact, I was certain of my own *insanity*. However, I knew what was real, and what wasn't. Then there was Walter. He shared my knowledge. We couldn't both be having the same, intensely detailed delusions.

So, if we really had done the things I remembered, and I was sure we had, someone was covering for us. Someone was hiding our handy work from the press, maybe even from the police. Perhaps that was why we hadn't been caught.

Was it possible that Walter was, without my knowledge, cleaning up after us? I couldn't imagine why. He wasn't afraid of repercussions. Even if he had been, why would he hide his actions from me? Surely when it came to eliminating evidence, two heads would be better than one.

Then I remembered Walter's strange mood. His sudden worry. What, I wondered, had been behind it?

I didn't know if I could convince Walter to tell me, but I had to try. I had no real choice in the matter.

Chaos

Some argue that we can't help it. None of it. Free will is a myth. A myth. They say that all of our choices are determined by our genetic makeup, our psychology, our likes and dislikes, the conditioning we underwent as children, antecedent events, and the laws of physics.

If this is so, then we do what we do merely because we could not do otherwise. We have no choice in the matter. And, no one can reasonably blame us.

None of us are free.

Police

It took some cajoling, but eventually Walter was willing to tell me the whole story. I want to tell you everything he shared with me. But first, I need to tell you this other thing.

I've been thinking about it a lot. I have a lot of time for self introspection, and rumination just at the moment. I've read a lot on the subject, and tried to draw connections. For some reason, I just don't seem to fit.

If I didn't know what I know now, I would probably assume that we remained free for so long because we didn't match the standard profile. Of course Walter's story (which I'll get to in a moment) negates that belief.

You see, all the literature says that I should have slowly escalated. I should have started, as a child, torturing and killing insects. Next would come small animals: 'possums, or cats and dogs. Then I should have physically abused a lover or two. Cruelty builds, minor tortures, then rape. Murder is the last step.

I don't fit. I went from complete passivity to homicidal behavior in one fell swoop. I'm simply one off, I guess.

Oh well.

Here's what Walter had to say.

He had been watching the girl all day. He had followed her through several shops. Watching intently as she perused objects on racks and shelves, but not buying anything. He had watched as she moved from place to place. He took careful note of how she moved, of her delicate, porcelain hands and how they caressed the things she hoped to possess. How her feet moved in small little rhythms.

He was watching her when it happened. He was planning. He was coveting, his eyes wild, mad, furry. The hand, gloved in leather fell on his shoulder, gently but firmly. Walter turned to see the cop meeting his gaze. The cop smiled.

"Not her, boy-o That one's off limits. Now scoot."

Walter looked at him with confusion, "What?".

"Pennies From heaven, Walter," was all the cop said as he walked out the door.

51

They knew. They knew who we were, and what we were doing. Somehow they knew. That cop, he had called Walter by name. And, they were letting us do it. They weren't stopping us. Somehow, we had been given a license to operate. A license to kill.

Justification

The girl. She was on her side, her back turned toward me. The sheet and slipped down to reveal her naked body. Her long black hair cascaded in a pool around her. I kept looking at the subtle curve of her hip, at the gentle slope of her shoulder. I wondered who she was. Silently she inhabited my bed. Silently she slept. From this angle, she could be anyone.

Walter walked into the room. He was pouring great handfuls of Cap'n Crunch into his hand, and stuffing them into the gaping maw of his mouth. His crunching was much too loud for this hour of the morning. I looked at him, questioning. As if to ask: whose this? But not wanting to say it out loud. Not wanting to rouse her from her slumber.

Wally, never the gentleman, swallowed and said: "So, what do ya think of her?"

"What?"

He had picked her up at some bar last night. He had brought her home. She was nineteen. A student at one of the local community colleges. Drunk already when Walter found her. He brought her to our house. When he was done with her, and she had passed out, he carried her into my bed, and placed her next to me. She was still passed out. Walter said I should give her a try. Then he walked out of the room.

I put my hand on her shoulder, and rolled her over. From this angle she was beautiful. Young, innocent looking. Clean. I ran my hand through her hair. I don't smile well. But then, you knew that.

Later, in the kitchen Walter asked me if she had woken up yet. No, I told him. He said we should get rid of her before she did. Dump her somewhere.

Just dump her? I asked. Just as she is?

Then Walter had another idea. We could keep her. For a little while, at least.

Walter went to get the duct tape, and one of my neck ties. This was his favorite way to bind and gag. It was his preferred *modus*, so to speak. It was his style.

As Walter bound her feet, I thought how I had climbed atop her. How I had

53

entered her. How she didn't move. Didn't wake up. Didn't know what I was doing to her. I look at her now, and she's beautiful. Helpless. Soft. Sleeping. Bound. Used. Beautiful. I could love her. I really could. You know how I mean. Forever, and forever, and forever. Happily ever after love. Real love. House and kids and two car garage with a picket fence love. I really could. I could love her forever, or for whatever passes for forever in this disposable post consumer world. But I knew that when we were finished with her, when we were bored of raping and torturing her, I would kill her. I would smear her blood all over my naked body. We might even cook parts of her, store some of her in the freezer like some grim casserole. Oh God, I feel like I'm falling. Just then, just knowing this, just looking at her there, beautiful and damned, I feel like I've slipped, tumbled over some precipice. Like I'm plummeting. Like the ground is rushing up to meet me at 9.8 meters per second, per second. Like I'm falling.

Did I tell you my name? We've been talking for so long, and I don't think I ever told you my name. It's Overby. John Overby. Write it down. Make sure you get it right. Remember it. I'm John Overby, Goddammitt, and I used to be human. I used to be real.

Walter had finished taping her hands, and was stuffing the folded tie in her mouth when she finally started to wake up. Her eyes were suddenly open and filled with panic. She was fighting, struggling against her bonds.

How Walter had her, her legs were apart. One ankle securely taped to each corner of the footboard. Her crotch was still wet, dripping from what I had done to her. Walter, he looked at me, smiled and undid his pants.

Unlike me, Walter has a convincing smile. One look at it and you're convinced that he's a lunatic. As I was walking out of the room Walter was climbing on top of her. He was gripping his erect penis in one hand, aiming for the soft wetness of her crotch.

Hitler wanted to be a painter. He couldn't get accepted to art school, and became a soldier instead. You already know the rest of that story. He slaughtered millions of people that he didn't even know. And in the evening he painted roses. So, you never can tell.

Overby wanted to be something too. I wanted to be, I don't remember what. But I know I had dreams of some sort. Vague aspirations. Something. You know the rest of that story too. I slaughter people that I don't even know. And in the evening I mix a mean martini.

Walter was zipping up his pants as he walked into the kitchen. I was pouring a glass of Johnny Walker Black down my throat. He slapped me on the back, and said it was my turn.

"What the hell", I said, "If I'm going to hell, I should at least enjoy the ride". That made Walter laugh. The room filled with that big booming laugh that could kill roses.

When I saw her eyes, big, round, wet, alive with terror, pain, shock, fear of death; when I saw her eyes I got very excited.

As I undid my pants she tried to scream through the silk Hermes tie that Walter had stuffed in her mouth. The sound that came was a muffled grunt.

Then I climbed on top of her. I forced my way inside her. As I took her I talked softly into her ear. I wanted to pull that tie out, and kiss her mouth, I said. I wanted to cut her throat and let her bleed to death, I said. I didn't know which I wanted to do first, I said. I very slowly, very calmly explained to her that I would be on top of her like this again, after she was dead.

Walter was watching from the doorway, and as I told her this he laughed.

Albert Fish liked to rape little girls. He liked to kill them, and eat their flesh. Albert, he traveled around the mid-west, cozying up to widows with young daughters. Albert had a pretty good thing going.

By the time I had finished, she had passed out. The fear and the stress were just too much. Shock can cause you to lose consciousness. Then it was Walter's turn again.

Walter told me once that as far as he was concerned, power was the only thing that mattered in this world. Power is everything.

What excites you? Sex? Sex is power. Money? Money is power too. Knowledge? It's power. A loaded gun? Guns are power. Big tits, a stack of fifties, elective office, a razor sharp blade. These things are all the same in the end. They are all just forms of power. Control. The ability to bend other to your will, by force or by coercion. An erect penis is power.

Walter was busy showing that poor doomed girl just how powerful he was. I went to get another drink.

Why were the police letting us do what we were doing? Not just letting us, but helping us? That we didn't make the papers suggested that someone was actively cleaning up after us. Covering up. Fixing it.

I had an idea why. But I wasn't certain. I needed more time to think, and I needed to talk to Walter about it. I settled down at the kitchen table, drink in hand, and started humming softly to myself while I waited for Walter to finish. Soon we'd have a lot of work to do.

Once Walter had had a job working for a motel. I forget which city it was in. It was one of the big ones. What Walter was paid to do was this: he went around to the other motel's in the neighborhood, and caused trouble. He knocked on the doors of people's rooms, then ran away. He carried around this loud air horn, and blew it in the middle of the night. He peeked in windows. He hung around the parking lot looking creepy. He approached people at the soda machine and asked them if their skin fit okay.

What this was all about was, customers would get scared. They would leave their unsafe motel, and some of them would end up at the motel that paid Walter's salary. It was a good scam. Walter would always have to be ready, to split if someone called the police. But that wasn't such a big concern. Most people wouldn't bother. Most of them would just pack up and move to another motel.

I kept thinking about that. That and the cop that had talked to Walter. "Pennies from Heaven" was running through my head.

After we dumped the girl's body in a lake, Walter and I went to get coffee.

Walter had blood on his sleeve. Not a lot of blood, but enough that I noticed it. It had seeped out of the tarp that we had wrapped her body in. It had stained his shirt. I didn't know if I should be worried about it or not. Given what I was thinking, I supposed I didn't have anything to be worried about. At least not yet.

Blue Beard

Most people don't know that the *inquisition* sponsored by the catholic church was really about money. Sure, they thought they were saving souls, torturing people into Christianity, but the real driving force was the profit motive.

The inquisitors, the torturers, could divide up the wealth of the heretics they had killed. Of course, the Pope got his cut. It was like a bloody pyramid scheme. Amway for zealots. The church needed money. It needed money because money is power. Everybody needs power.

Walter was sipping his coffee. The people crowded into little booths around us had no idea that they were within spitting distance of two homicidal killers. Two psychopaths of the first order. They were enjoying grand slam breakfasts, and greasy cheeseburgers in Denny's, for God's sake. Obviously they were safe here.

I had poured too much cream in my coffee. It was milky, like semen, and lukewarm. I kept looking around for the waitress to come back by, so I could get her to add some hot coffee to my cup. Unfortunately, she seemed to have disappeared from the face of the earth like some Latin American dissident. I had very little hope of her return. Other people around me were in the same boat. We needed a waitress, but none was evident.

The first pirates worked for governments. Britain would finance pirates, who would attack and plunder French ships. France would finance pirates who would attack and plunder British ships. Of course the King always got his cut of the loot.

These pirates, although not officially part of the Navy, worked under the protection of the government. It was standard procedure. It made the sea lanes unsafe for the wrong people. Piracy made governments stronger. Everybody wins. The crown grows in power, the pirates get rich, and the average person is held down in their proper place.

Walter poured more sugar into his coffee. He couldn't get enough sugar. He liked to drink, what looked to be a cup of sugar with a little puddle of coffee in it.

I preferred just a little cream. Not too much. I was looking into my cup, not talking, when the waitress walked by the table moving quickly. I tried to draw her attention, but failed miserably.

Walter was talking again. I wasn't really paying attention. I was busy thinking. I was thinking about the girl we had just disposed of. How her body, wrapped in a plastic tarp that had leaked just a bit, had tumbled through the air, flipping over and over aging as we dropped her from the highway overpass to the cold water below.

I was thinking about the lawn. Actually about the boy I paid to mow the lawn. I was wondering if he had seen anything odd, anything he might mention to his parents. I was wondering if we should dispose of him, like the girl.

I was thinking about the police. And about pirates. And about Pauline, my little wounded bird. And about Walter. About what Walter had done before he met me. About what Walter would do after he moved out of my house. Was I, I wondered, Walter's first partner in crime; or just one in a string.

But mostly I was thinking about that damned waitress, and my now cold cup of coffee that needed her attention.

"That's next, of course. But first we have to find her."

I had no idea what he was talking about. That first night, when I met him at that party, I thought I had Walter figured out completely. I had been so fucking wrong.

"What did you say?" I asked.

"I said: I thought it worked out pretty well with that girl. I said: we should do that again. One of us can drag some drunk bitch home. Then we can use her for a few days, then dump her."

People at the next booth had heard. I was certain of that. They were looking at us. Eyes wide, filled with shock, confusion. I looked directly at the man, and blew him a kiss. He suddenly found his plate of eggs incredibly interesting.

"Well, you're better at picking them up."

"Yeah," he said, "I am."

I told him that if that's what he wanted to do, he should go ahead. I wouldn't complain.

These days I didn't think about the things that had worried me before. B.W. Before Walter. The mounting tensions. The troubles that faced humanity. The steady onrush of oblivion, of destruction. The coming end of civilization. I didn't worry about the death of humanity. I was no longer one of them. Finally, I was one of the alligator people. Without empathy. Without sympathy. I was the way the world ends. Not with a bang, or a whimper. But with me. And I was starting to be happy about it.

But I still had questions. And it was time to share them with Walter.

When it finally happens, when the sun goes, our atmosphere will burn off. All of that oxygen will flash-fry everything on the planets surface. We will all get terminal sun burn.

Answers

So, if the world ends, would you care? Would you even notice? What would it mean? Okay, so no more *Survivor*. No more *Fear Factor*. But, why should that bother you? No more *Big Brother*, no more *Friends*, no more *Wheel of Fortune*. But really, why do you care?

It's like these people. They watch those videos. You know the one's. *Faces of Death*, and the like. Real death caught on film. Industrial accidents. Car wrecks. Carnival ride accidents. House fires. Anything that someone could get on video. These are people mangled. People broken. Beaten. Raped. Decapitated. Burned. Drowned. Shot. Stabbed. Killed. This is death. Real, live death. And it's all in color. It's for real, each blood soaked detail, every torn flesh nuance, each gore drenched minute. And they eat it up. They can't live without it.

China is televising their executions now. Three a week. Murderers, rapists, child molesters, repeat felons, political dissidents, religious fanatics. They put 'em down in ways that are only considered humane in the worst parts of the world. Madame Guillotine would be proud. Torquemeda would giggle gleefully. And a huge television audience lines up to watch.

So, the end of the world means no more reality TV. No bang. No whimper. Just white noise. Static as all the satellite stations go off the air. That's the sound people fear most.

Television is just another drug. It paralyzes the mind, numbs the senses, shuts out the real world. Like morphine, or cocaine, or anonymous sex, or gambling, or obsessive hand washing, TV is just another addiction. The addiction to the cathode ray tube is both physical and psychological. Take it away from someone you know, and see what happens.

I haven't turned on my TV in months. I don't need to anymore.

I told Walter what I thought about the police. I told him about pirates. He laughed at me. But, as he laughed I thought I caught sight of something in his eyes. Something that said I could be right. Something that said he'd need to check it out.

I reminded him about that motel he had worked for. That clinched it. He had some questions to ask. He needed to check a few things. He'd see me, he said, when he knew for sure. He knew just where to look for the answers he needed.

I wanted to know how he planned on finding these things out. He said it was better for me not to know. I didn't like that much, but I said I guessed I could live with it. For now.

Walter walked out the door. I wouldn't see him again for almost two weeks. By then it would be too late.

When Walter came back, he would have a lot to tell me. But before I lay all of that out, I need to tell you a bit about what I experienced in that time. A lot of it didn't seem particularly important at the time, but later it would all seem to fit together. Like one of those puzzles with a thousand disconnected pieces. At first it all seems like a pile of nothing. Like just a bunch of random picture bits. It's only after you start to assemble it that something coherent begins to peek out at you. Life is like that, sometimes.

Questions

Waking up. The sun coming through my window, throwing its unfiltered light on my face. Throwing its heat across my skin. I hate it. I barely see the day, and I don't need to be reminded so rudely that I am a creature of the night.

Some fish live so far down in the ocean, never approaching the surface, never seeing any light, that they have no need for eyes. Living in total darkness, evolution has stolen the ability for sight from them. Their skin is translucent, almost completely see through. Sun light would most likely kill them. It hurts me.

When Walter left, he left her behind. This girl, so like the first one he had brought home: beautiful and terrified. I wasn't sure what I should do with her. I could have just killed her, then hidden the body until Walter returned. I knew that I'd need his help to dispose of her. But, I kind of liked her. I didn't want to see her go just yet.

I was starting to think of her as a pet. I supposed that if I didn't want her to die right away, I should try to feed her something. At least get her to take some water.

To do that I'd have to remove the gag from her mouth. I didn't think she'd scream. It had been nearly a day since she tried to make any sort of noise beyond a frightened grunt. Maybe, I thought, I could give her a bath. She was so utterly terrified of me that I doubted she would struggle much if I untied her.

I could hold her in the bath tub, and quickly wash her. I decided that, just to keep her completely docile, I would rape her again. Then I would tell her how she would be tortured if she tried to get away. Then I would give her a bath, and force her to eat something.

She was tied on her back. Duct tape held her wrists together behind her torso. More duct tape held her ankles to the bed posts. A very lovely Armani tie was stuffed in her mouth. I loved that tie. It was the finest silk; soft and shiny. Damn, that was a great tie.

She seemed to be asleep as I approached her. I slipped off my pants, and began to climb on top of her. I was hoping that I could start before she woke up.

All this reminded me of one night Walter and I had broken into this girl's apartment. We had beaten her, and tied her up just like this. We had both used her. I was in the middle of fucking her again when I realized that she was already dead. I could barely finish.

With that in mind, I forced my erect penis inside her. She didn't stir. So, I reached out and slapped her face, hard. Her eyes snapped open. Good.

It's not that I have a problem fucking a dead girl. Necrophilia. What the hell. I just want to know that she's dead before hand. I don't want to be surprised.

After I was done, she was nearly catatonic. I had been rougher than usual. I had done things to her that I normally didn't do. I had forced things inside her. A beer bottle. A wooden spoon. A toy soldier. Anything I could think of. I had beaten her a bit. I had raped her ass. I held my knife to her throat. I had told her things. I told her all of the lovely fun we would have together if she tried to escape.

I did all of this to keep her docile, so I could go through with my plan.

I climbed off of her, and went to start the bath water.

Did I tell you that I was born in the winter? Yeah. I guess I did.

I began to fill the tub with hot water. I thought about it for a minute. Then I added some bubbles, and some moisturizer to the water. I thought she might need it. I placed my knife, huge, sharp and phallic on the counter next to the sink. I checked the water temperature again. It seemed about right. I didn't want it too hot. She would be sore from everything I had done to her. I made sure that I had the proper soaps, shampoo, and clean towels at my disposal. Then I stopped the water, and went to get her.

She looked like she had slipped back into unconsciousness, while I was preparing the bath. I leaned close to her face, and began to speak.

At first she gave no sign of hearing me. I pinched one of her nipples between my thumb and forefinger, and gave a vicious twist. That did it. She was awake.

I told her again about the price of attempting to escape. I told her how I could gut her, but still keep her alive for hours. I told her how I would rape her, after I slit her abdomen. How it would feel, being fucked with her viscera hanging out of the gaping wound where her stomach should be. I told her about her eyes. How I could cut them out of their orbits without severing the optic nerve. Her eyes would be out of her head, but she'd still be able to see.

I told her all of this as a warning. I didn't want to do any of it. Yet. I wanted to keep her around until Walter returned. See, I knew that without Walter I would get bored, and go out hunting on my own. I didn't want to do that. I was afraid to.

So, I needed her. I needed her to keep me company. To give me something to do. I needed to give her a bath, because she was starting to stink. In a few days the smell would be unbearable. I should have just killed her then.

I slowly untied her. I was watching for any sign that she was about to fight or run. She gave no resistance.

Women are dangerous. Ships are always named after women. It only makes sense. If you're a sailor, you love your ship. You care for her constantly. She requires all of your attention. But you can never really control her. If you mistreat her, you're dead. That's all there is to it. If you forget to take care of her needs, she'll kill you.

Hurricanes also get female names.

So I carried her, half catatonic and limp, into the bathroom. I lowered her into the soapy water. I did this gently. I did it carefully. I should have held her head under until she stopped breathing. I should have slit her throat.

Instead I soaped her body. I paid careful attention to cleaning every inch of her. I admit, I cleaned some parts a bit more diligently than others. I may have lingered a bit longer in certain areas than in others.

As I was soaping her breasts, something odd happened. She smiled at me. Sweetly. The smile stretched all the way to her eyes. For some reason I believed this smile.

When I had washed and rinsed every inch of her, I told her to stand. I toweled her off. I took her left wrist, and twisted it behind her back. I was under the illusion that I was in complete control.

Holding her wrist tightly behind her, I pushed her out of the bathroom. I pushed her back to the bed, and shoved her down on it. Not too hard, though. She was so fucking pretty. So fucking small.

I asked, if I brought her food, would she eat or would I have to force feed her. She'd eat, she said.

I told her to lie down, so I could tie her. I would undo her hands so she could eat, but while I was getting the food she needed to be bound. She complied sweetly. She lay back, and spread her legs wide for me to bind them. She sat up, and crossed her wrists behind her back while I wrapped them in tape. She opened her mouth, ready for the gag. I told her not to bother.

By that point I was fucked, even if I didn't know it yet.

In the kitchen I busied myself opening a can of soup, and finding the saltines. I warmed the soup on the stove, and arranged the crackers around a plate. I had to search to find a clean spoon. Finally I gave up and washed one.

I poured the soup in a bowl, and balanced it on the plate. I dropped the spoon in the hot soup, and carried it back into the bedroom.

I placed the plate and bowl on the dresser, and helped her sit up so I could untie her hands. When her hands were free, I placed the plate on the bed between her open legs. She grabbed the spoon, and began to rapidly fill her mouth with steaming soup.

I told her to slow down, or she'd make herself sick. She slowed down a little, but not much. I watched her eat, and when she was done I took the bowl away.

She dutifully crossed her wrists behind her back, and I taped them together again.

As I picked up the plate and bowl I heard her say: "Thank you."

I didn't respond.

The next day I fixed her spaghetti, and we went through much the same routine.

This time, after she ate, after her hands were firmly taped together, I pulled off my pants and climbed on top of her. As I was entering her, she whispered in my ear: "You didn't have to tie me up for this."

That night I went out for groceries. I told her to lie still while I was gone. She suggested that I should put her gag back in. In case, she said. Not that she would think of screaming, she told me. But just in case she got scared while I was gone. I did as she suggested.

At the store, I was pushing my cart. Looking over the items on the shelves. Trying to decide which things I actually needed. The only things currently in my cart were duct tape, apples, and a bottle of gin.

I didn't recognize the man. He was older and nicely dressed. He had a distinguished look to him. I had noticed him following me but had paid little mind.

As I turned down the coffee and tea isle, suddenly he was standing face to face with me.

"Are you on vacation?"

"What?" I asked him.

"You haven't been working. You boys were doing so well. Why don't you get back to work?"

The last seemed more like an order, than a question. I told him he should fuck himself. Then I pushed past him, and quickly headed down the isle. He called after me that I should get back to work.

The following day it was soup again. My culinary skills are extremely limited, and I had already run out of dinner choices. The soup in the bowl was too hot. She was waiting for it to cool before she started eating.

I was looking at her sitting there, naked, beautiful, intent on her soup. I thought we were something like *La Belle et La Bete*. Hostage and monster having dinner together. It was all so cute; so French. We were like some lovely fairy tale. At least, my warped mind seemed to think so.

I don't believe in free will. Not at all. I think that we are all slaves to physics, and genetics, and conditioning. We have no choice in how we behave. We act as nature demands. The horrible things I have done: I couldn't have done otherwise. I'm certain of that.

It was at that moment that the bowl, and all of its nearly boiling contents came down on my head. My eyes stung from the hot, salty liquid. I saw pinpricks of light bobbing before my eyes. I was just starting to shake my head, to clear it, when the plate crashed over my skull.

She was already up. The tape around her ankles must have been loose. She must have been quietly working at it, because she was able to pull it off so effortlessly.

I was on the floor, on my side, rubbing at my eyes. I felt the stab of her foot as she kicked me in the gut. She kicked hard. All of the breath flew out of me.

I started to cough. She was gone.

By the time I got up, she was only a memory. The front door was standing open. I looked out. I looked both directions down the street, but I couldn't see her anywhere.

I quickly closed and locked the door. I found my knife, and held it tightly. This, I thought, is the end. I should have killed her when I had the chance. Now she'd find a cop, and soon my door would fly off the hinges.

They'd fire tear gas canisters through the windows. They would storm in wearing riot gear, and carrying automatic weapons. I would crumple in a hail of bullets.

No one remembers Melvin Purvis. John Dillinger was coming out of a theater, after seeing a movie with his girlfriend. Dillinger was the most wanted man in America. As he walked out onto the street, an FBI agent named Melvin Purvis shot Dillinger dead.

Everyone remembers Dillinger. No one remembers poor Melvin.

People will remember me. The cop, the one that shoots me down in my living room will be little more than a foot note in history.

Dillinger's girlfriend dropped the dime. She turned him in for the reward.

I was thinking this when the knock came. I was wishing that I had a gun, instead of just the knife. I walked to the door, ready to face my demise. Ready to have my body torn apart by flying lead moving at nearly the speed of sound.

As I opened the door I was shocked by what I saw. It was the girl. She was in hand cuffs, and a dirty rag was stuffed in her mouth.

A cop had hold of her. He said: "Here. I think this belongs to you." He shoved her into the house, and turned to walk away. As he did, he called out that I should get back to work.

I looked at her, her eyes glassy and moist. I pulled back my fist, and swung. It connected with her jaw. Solid. She crumpled on the floor.

I picked her up and got to work tying her to the bed. This time she wouldn't find her bonds so easy to slip. This time she wouldn't find me so easy to manipulate.

After she was returned to her place on the bed, I made myself some toast and coffee. I had a lot of work ahead of me, and I'd need all the energy I could get.

I was going to show her that the promises I had made about attempts to escape were true.

Bodies in Motion

The unread newspapers had begun to pile up in the kitchen. I never even unfolded them. If I were more socially conscious, I would have recycled them.

But, I had a better use for all of that paper.

She was awake now. I had raped her again. I had beaten her a bit. I had cut her. Just a few small slices across her stomach and face. I had rubbed a little salt in the wounds. I had barely gotten started.

The phone rang. I picked it up.

The voice on the other end said that I should tell Walter to stop asking questions.

"Who is this?" I asked.

We didn't want the answers, the voice assured me. We should just get back to work. No more questions. Then the voice was gone, and I was holding the phone for no reason.

I wondered for a minute if there had really been anyone on the phone, or if I had just imagined it. I put the phone down, and got back to work.

The doctor who invented the Lobotomy won a Nobel prize. He performed his procedure with a pointed, icepick-like instrument. He would drill a little hole in the patients skull, poke out portions of the frontal lobe. This was considered a humane way to deal with the insane and the mentally retarded. This was a great leap forward in medicine.

Thinking about this had given me an idea. But that was for later.

To really soak up any amount of blood, newsprint works best if it is at least four layers thick. Less than that and the blood will seep right through. Blood, and other protein stains like semen, are very difficult to remove.

A wire brush and a bit of peroxide can help, but even when it's invisible to the naked eye, the stain will still show up with Luminol and a black light.

Your best bet is simply to burn sheets and clothes that have become stained. Of course, I had only recently begun to think about such things.

After she was dead, I decided to store that body until Walter got home. She wouldn't fit in the freezer, so I had to cut her up. I placed her in the bathtub, which I had lined with plastic, to control the mess.

I used the hacksaw, a cleaver, and a butcher knife. It only took about two hours to reduce her to manageable pieces. I wrapped the pieces in plastic, stored her in the freezer, and went about cleaning up my mess.

With her gone, I didn't have much to do. I had been afraid of that. I knew that if Walter didn't get back soon, I'd go hunting on my own. That was dangerous.

Home From The Hill

Walter had taught me that the most dangerous part of what we did was the choosing. Once you know who your victim is, you can plan, and look for ways to avoid trouble. Once you have them, you're home free.

But, the wrong choice can spell disaster. If you're wrong about the sort of person that you've chosen, no amount of planning will save you.

Those young college girls who look so soft and defenseless, they know judo. They carry mace. They've been to all those rape prevention classes where they teach you to use your keys as a weapon, and scream fire.

The little old lady with the house full of cats, she has a .38 in her purse. She has an alarm system with a buried, dedicated, un-cuttable phone line directly to the police.

The middle-aged socialite, she's killed three husbands, and won't have any problem with you. They'll take you out like you were nothing. Squash you like a bug.

Even with all of that in mind, I decided to give it a try. I was lonely. Walter had been gone more than a week. The girl had been gone awhile, too. She was still around, but being in little pieces in the freezer she just wasn't much fun any more.

I decided that I would be very careful. I decided that I would take my time, and not rush things. I would use diligence, caution, and patience as my weapons. I would be smooth.

I was sitting on the couch, thinking. I was using this time to plan. I thought that I needed to lay the whole thing out in my head before I started. Then, after I had it all worked out in every minute detail, then I could set about choosing my victim.

While I was relaxed there, half in shadow, something was happening outside. I didn't know it at the time, but someone had been very busy. Someone was as anxious for me to get back to work, as I was.

When that cop brought the girl back to me I thought it was just luck. I didn't ask questions. I knew that something was going on, that someone was protecting us. But it was too much for me to think about.

Walter was putting that particular puzzle together, and I had decided to wait for answers. So, when I heard the knocking sound on the door, I had no idea what was coming. I couldn't have known.

I rose from my place on the couch, walked to the door, and opened it.

Joan of Arc was a schizophrenic cross-dresser. Martin Luther was an angry anti-Semite. John Calvin was a power mad murderer. Thomas Jefferson raped a slave girl. Who are your heroes?

Outside the door, setting on the step was a package. About the size of a shoebox, wrapped in brown paper, it bore a tag with my name on it. It was signed "A Friend." I carried it inside and closed the door behind me.

I opened the package. Inside was a medium sized manila envelope. On top of that was a gun. Black, slick, it was a Ruger 9mm.

I picked up the gun and looked at it. I turned it over in my hands. I examined it closely. I had held guns before, but had never owned one. Walter had several. He didn't have one like this though.

I set the gun aside, and picked up the envelope. It was sealed with wax. I tore the end open, and dumped out the contents.

There was a black and white, eight by ten photo of a young girl. She had long, wavy hair and big almond shaped eyes. She was very pretty, but not beautiful in any conventional way.

There were also several sheets of paper. On these were typed information about the girl. Where she lived, her schedule, the routes she took to and from work, the layout of her apartment, the types of locks she had. Everything. Her whole existence was laid out on those few sheets of paper. Everything one would need to stalk her, to catch her, to kill her.

This I found troublesome. This was stranger by far than any of the other things that had occurred in the past. Yet, I was almost certain that I would act on the information that had been handed to me. I would have to. The need was growing too great to ignore. The desire was overwhelming.

It would be best, I knew, to wait for Walter's return. But, I was afraid that I wouldn't be able to do that.

I decided to wait until the next night to make any sort of decision about it. With that thought in mind, I went to the kitchen and poured myself a drink. I sat at the table and enjoyed the cold gin.

After a few minutes I walked back into the other room, retrieved the gun and carried it back to the kitchen with me. I set it on the table, and looked at it. I stared at it. I let my eyes play over ever contour, every facet of its texture. I contemplated it.

I picked it up and checked to see if it was loaded. It was. The clip was full of hollow point bullets. These I knew would shatter on impact creating several small, jagged pieces of shrapnel. The torn bits of lead would shred their way through soft tissue and muscle. These were bullets designed to kill. These were bullets designed to destroy a human animal.

I held the gun in my hand, felt its weight, held it out in front of me as if aiming at some unseen person, then placed it back on the table.

The gun seemed to stare at me. To bore a hole into me. It had weight, some psychological density. It had a realness that was difficult to comprehend. It was just so fucking there. I could feel its gravity from the other room.

Return

Really, if you had to choose, freezing is the best way to die. Sure, the cold hurts. It hurts quite a bit at first. But after awhile, you stop being cold. As your body temperature drops, the air feels warm in relation to you. You feel warm, and sleepy, and mildly drugged. Then you drift off to sleep.

Not a bad way to go. If you could choose.

I was just waking up when I heard the noise. Someone was opening the door. I sat bolt upright on the couch, and groped around on the floor for the gun where I had left it when I finally drifted off to sleep. My hand found the gun, and gripped it tightly. Its weight, its heft was reassuring in my hand. It felt good.

I leaned outward from the couch, holding the gun in both hands, pointing it directly at the door, my index finger lightly on the trigger. I was ready. I was going to open a large hole in the front of whoever walked through the door. I didn't do that, though.

The person entering my home unannounced was Walter. I began to tremble. For a moment, upon seeing him, I felt as though I would weep. I didn't do that either.

Instead I dropped the gun. It landed with a thud. Walter had a large, frightening smile bolted to his face. He looked as if he was happier than he had ever been.

I asked him what he had found out. He told me that he needed sleep before he got into it. Walter made his way to the kitchen, poured himself a stiff drink, gulped it down, then found a spot on the floor. He stretched his bulk out, and was asleep as soon as he closed his eyes.

He would sleep there for nearly sixteen hours. When he awoke, he would share quite the strange tale.

I wouldn't sleep in that time. Mostly what I did was watch Walter sleep.

Walter's Story

We live in a society that glorifies violence. Our sports are built around war. Football, the most popular sport in this country, is a simple war game. Soldiers, wearing armor of sorts, fight to make gains on the field of battle. They do so violently.

Television is filled with stories of violence. Cops and robbers. Drug dealers and murderers. Rapists and thieves. These are the stories we tell to our children.

Our movies are filled with violence. Our music even is becoming nothing but a glorification of violence. We are a civilization designed to create killing machines. Machines like me.

Walter told me what he had found out, but not how he had found it out.

What Walter told me was this:

We were not alone. Although we had been operating in the dark, others had been watching out for us. Others had been helping us. Protecting us. We were part of a plan. We were official. We were unknowingly working for the government.

They needed us. We gave them power. Those in charge had decided long ago that people were easier to control when they lived in constant fear. So they had begun a program to locate natural predators, and to secretly cultivate them. They gave us protection, steered us quietly, and gave us room to work. In this way the average person could be more readily subjugated.

And we weren't the only ones. All over the country others were doing exactly what we had been doing. All of it sanctioned. We were the secret police. We were the hidden force. We were the hand of power.

Of course, we were disposable. There were plenty like us. If we should die, or go to prison others would simply fill our place. Others would be protected. That was the way it had always worked.

When Bundy, or Fish had to be sacrificed, a replacement was easy to find. Hell, we were breeding monsters.

Onward

It was important, Walter said, that no one in power ever know that we had found this out. We should go on as we had before. We should continue to work. To kill. To destroy. As if nothing had changed.

So that was precisely what we did. We cut a swath through the world. We tried our best to destroy civilization, to rid the planet of human life. At night I would dream of cities aflame. I could see the death of humanity, and I longed for it.

Then everything changed.

We started by acting on the information left at my door step. It was easy. It didn't have to hunt, search, or plan. We just killed her.

Then we chose another victim. And another. We were the reaper. We killed everyone and everything we could.

Then, suddenly, without notice, it all came crashing down. Everything we had done was aimed precisely at the one moment when it would all end. That moment came as a massive shock to us both. To Walter perhaps more than me. Walter.

Apres Moi, Le Deluge

Walter. Walter. Walter. Walter. I say his name. I say it again and again. I say it out loud, and I inscribe it on the page. I scream it to the trees. I have carved it into the earth in letters four feet high. Yet it doesn't seem real. I cannot make him materialize, no matter how emphatically I shout his name. Walter.

Walter was gone. Dead. A memory. But wait.

We had been working hard. For weeks we had killed, and killed. Then we had killed some more. Walter and I both figured that if we were being protected, we should just go all out. So we did. Then it all went wrong.

We had come in through the front door. Walter had worked his magic on the lock, and we had walked into the dark house. We had done this hundreds of times before. It was always easy.

We didn't even bother to survey the house. We just made our way clumsily through the darkness. Walter slammed his thigh into an end table, knocking over a lamp in the process. He laughed out loud at this. I smiled, unconcerned. We were well on our way to the bedroom where she would be softly sleeping. The girl, we were certain, had no idea what she was in for. We were coming to visit her. She would, very soon, get her first real look at terror. Her first true view of fear. Her first real and personal knowledge of death.

When we came to the bedroom door, I noticed right away that the bed was empty. This was wrong. I caught the movement from the corner of my eye. Something streaked out of the room. I turned just in time to see the girl standing there, naked except for the gun clenched tightly in both hands. The huge barrel stared out at me.

Walter came rushing past me, toward the girl. The gun erupted in a flash of flame and sound. Walter, as if punched hard in the gut, doubled over, and crumpled onto the floor.

The girl was already gone. Running from the room. Fleeing the house. Walter's blood was everywhere. He was trying to speak, so I leaned down and put my ear close to his mouth. His hand softly touched my face. It left a small smear of blood. A bubble of blood and saliva popped against my ear as he spoke.

Not real. Not real. Not real. I'm not real.

This was all he said over and over as the red and blue lights began to play violently across the white walls of the bedroom. The blood seemed almost to glow in the swirling, flashing lights. The Walter was gone.

I didn't even bother to run.

Something Like An Epilogue

I'm alone now. Not really alone, but apart. Watched very closely. Medicated. This place isn't real. Not in the way that other places are real. Nothing here is what it seems to be.

They call them doctors. Doctors, and psychiatrists, and therapists, and nurses, and orderlies. They call this a hospital. An institution. An asylum. They watch me, question me, and medicate me. I live in white walled rooms with lots of natural light and green plants.

I am surrounded by vegetables, droolers, bed wetters, and Freudian messes. And they don't believe me. None of it, they assure me, happened.

All of the things I've told you are, in their considered medical opinion, dreams. Hallucinations. Products of my fevered imagination. The creation of my overworked mind. Bad chemicals.

No, they say, I wasn't found in some woman's bedroom standing over the bloody corpse of my dead friend. No, my freezer wasn't filled with frozen delicacies consisting of the lovingly dismembered bodies of young women. No, I hadn't really racked up the biggest body count in my state's history. I only thought that. I only thought that because my wiring had short circuited. I only believe these things because of bad chemicals. It is just my imagination. These things only seemed to happen. They were only apparently real.

I am, they say, quite mad.

They wont let me read the papers. I can't watch television. No radio. I am provided with pre-recorded music. All of it meant to be soothing. All of it meant to lull me into a fugue: a dream state in which I can forget my madness.

Pills. They bring pills in a rainbow of colors, and I dutifully choke them down. They reassure me. They stroke my ego. Someday, they tell me, I can go home.

But I don't believe it. They will never let me out of this cage. They know. They know quite well what I would do if they set me free. They know what I've done. They know. They know it's the truth.

I wonder sometimes. I wonder what became of Walter's body. Probably buried in an unmarked pauper's grave somewhere. Forgotten. That doesn't seem right. It doesn't seem fair.

Escape? Sure. I've thought about it. But I'm watched much too closely for that. I can't get out of here on my own power. And, there is no one left who would want to help me. The world wants me in my little pen. I suppose I belong here. That's okay. I don't mind. It won't be long now anyway.

Soon I really will be alone. The tensions are still mounting outside that wall. The world is still reaching for the light of oblivion. It is still disintegrating, crumbling, collapsing. Falling. They'll destroy themselves out there. They have to. They can't help it, you see. It's all a matter of bad chemicals, and short-circuited wiring.

When the world goes up, I'll be safe behind these white walls. Where I belong. Soon. I think.

They're coming now. They have a variety of pills for me. They want to soothe my poor, broken mind. They want to save me. I have to take them. I have to be a good boy, and wait patiently.

I understand. I can wait it out. I can wait them out. I can wait: forever. Time, you see, is on my side. I can out last this world, and the next. None of us are free.

When it does happen, I'll be here, waiting.

That's all I wanted to tell you. Sweet dreams. Good night. So long. Farewell. See you in the funny papers. See you at the end of the world.

Printed in the United Kingdom
by Lightning Source UK Ltd.
122445UK00003B/541/A